SADIE, SADIE, P.I. LADY

"A woman is like a tea bag: you cannot tell how strong she is until you put her in hot water."
~Nancy Reagan -

SADIE, SADIE, P.I. LADY

A Stairwell Murder Mystery

Michelle Gabriel

To Judy + Harry
always with
good wishes,
Michelle Gabriel
~2014~

ISBN: 1500224332
ISBN 13: 9781500224332
Library of Congress Control Number: 2014911965
CreateSpace Independent Publishing Platform
North Charleston, South Carolina

PROLOGUE

I'm ambivalent about being called Sadie Sadie, P.I. Lady, even in jest. My name's not Sadie, it's Sonja, Sonja Maven. And I'm not a P.I., certainly not a private investigator.

The Sadie part is what my husband Milt and grown children, Frannie and Paul, often call me because of what they perceive to be my likeness to my mother-in-law Sadie. She liked to poke around a bit in other people's business and, they point out, I tend to do the same. They attach the P.I. part because of what they say is an overwhelming affinity to become permanently involved, persistently intrigued, or their favorite, positively insane, in the process. It has become their little joke, or comic relief, for all the stress they insist I give them with my, um, passionate involvement.

The Sadie part's okay. The P.I. designation isn't.

Like my mother-in-law, I'm outgoing, naturally curious and enjoy helping people. I also believe that you have to know a little about the people you want to help before you actually offer help.

On the other hand, the P.I. private investigator reference couldn't be further from the truth. I'm a 62-year old housewife in Brooklyn, of medium height, relatively sound mind and adequately sound body.

The only investigating I've ever done has been helping my neighbors find lost keys, missing mail and once, a strange noise coming from a bathtub when a visiting grandchild pushed a squeeze toy up the faucet. Obviously, my so-called investigations are pretty benign stuff. At least it has been until a few weeks ago during my little, uh, run in with the police, a killer and a very dead body.

CHAPTER ONE

It started innocently enough. I was walking back to the apartment building where Milt and I live, carrying a heavy bag of groceries. It was a chilly Wednesday morning, not unusual for an East Coast March. My intention had been to just buy milk, eggs and a loaf of bread. The heavy part happened when I saw the two-for-one sale on Milt's favorite ice cream, mint chocolate chip.

I heard a commotion as soon as I stepped inside the building. Several neighbors were huddled in the lobby near the mailboxes, shouting to be heard.

"What's going on?" I blurted out. "Someone win the lottery?"

The neighbors stared back at me. Mr. Fisher, a long time tenant, pointed towards a notice taped to the wall. I moved closer and read.

> *"This building is in the process of being sold. The new owners have indicated their plan to convert all apartments into condos. A formal letter of intent will be sent within the week. Sol Rubenstein, Rubenstein Proprieties Inc.*

This was not good. Our six-story residential apartment building is home to many seniors who moved in several years ago when rent control was offered. They have enjoyed that little perk ever since. Giving up rent control and having to either move or buy into expensive condos were not appropriate options.

"Who put this up?" I asked. "I didn't see any notice an hour ago when I left for the market."

"Some man I never saw before," Esther Pinsky, an octogenarian who lived next door to us on the fourth-floor shouted. "I came down to get my mail. I got off the elevator and here's this big brute taping something on the wall. Probably one of Sol Rubenstein's henchmen."

An ageless wonder, Mrs. Pinsky was barely five feet tall. Making me, at five feet four inches feel like a giant. She was also highly opinionated and, bless her heart, very excitable.

"He's kicking us out of our homes," she continued ranting. "And his own father living right here in this building too. We have to do something, Mrs. Maven."

"Yes, of course we do. And we will." I said. "This came out of the blue and I'm as shocked as you are. I'll call Sol. I've met him once or twice when he visited his father. I'll tell him we're upset. I'll insist that he come here and talk to us." I said this as if I really thought I had that much power to order our landlord to appear at my command. I didn't, but it felt like the right thing to say at the moment.

I started to say more but was suddenly interrupted as Helen Brunner, another tenant, bumped my shoulder as she pushed past me. Without a word or an apology, she walked straight to the notice and began reading.

"Isn't that something," I said, moving closer to her. "The selling of the building's like a bombshell dropped on us."

She stared at me a moment, then without a word, turned and walked away.

I stood there with my mouth open. Admittedly, we didn't know each other well, but still, I was taken aback by her behavior. Before I could react, Mrs. Pinsky let out a cry, placing her hand over her chest.

Fearing a heart attack, I rushed to her. "Mrs. Pinsky, are you all right? Do you need a doctor? Should we call 911?"

"No doctor." She answered slowly. "I'm fine, just angry. I shouldn't get so excited, but this whole thing is terrible."

Mrs. Pinsky could be tough as nails, but at that moment, leaning against the wall for support, she looked frail and vulnerable.

"Look," I said gently. "I don't like this either, but Sol owns the building. He has every right to sell. Still, we shouldn't think the worst. Maybe I can get him to delay the sale or at least offer something to help us through this." Of course I had no idea what Sol would or wouldn't do. I just knew I had to attempt to do something.

"I'll walk you to your apartment. Then I'll talk to Milt. He might have some ideas that will help. Maybe there's a loophole in Brooklyn's rent control laws."

Truth be told, I wasn't so thrilled with the selling of the building either. Our kids had been after us for years to move to Long Island to be closer to them. We were resisting. It wasn't that we don't like to see our children and grandchildren. Of course we do. However Milt and I also like our independence. Milt had been an information technology engineer for an East Coast computer start-up. The company did well and Milt was able to retire a few years ago. Since then we enjoyed the flexibility of being able to travel, take walks or go to a movie whenever we wanted. We love family visits, however, we also appreciate the peace and quiet when the kids return home. Unless there was a way to convince Sol not to go through with the sale, the kids would up their resolve to have us move. While we could continue to refuse, it would invite countless arguments and hurt feelings. In the end, we would feel we had little choice but to agree to their plan for us to move.

I felt moisture seeping through the bag. Milt's ice cream! I walked Mrs. Pinsky back to her apartment as fast as I could without actually pushing her. I stayed long enough to make sure she was okay, then quickly went to my apartment.

"Sol's selling the building," I shouted as I opened the door. I walked into the kitchen and placed the soggy ice cream cartons into the freezer and the rest of the groceries in the refrigerator. I found Milt in the bedroom fixing the closet door.

"What?" Milt stopped what he was doing, took off his glasses and turned to face me. Just under six feet and a little stocky, his eyes held the same twinkle they had the day we met more than forty years ago.

I told him about the flyer, adding the neighbor's comments and my concerns. "Isn't there anything we can do? You were an engineer. Don't you have connections? Someone on the city council, or maybe the planning commission?"

Milt sat on the bed. "I haven't spoken to anyone on the planning commission for years. I don't know if those guys still work there or if they'd even remember me. Sadie, I know you want to help the neighbors, but we don't have all the facts. We don't even know when the building will actually be sold or who's buying it."

I started pacing. Milt didn't react to situations impulsively as I did. It was the engineer in him. He needed all the facts. I needed to worry about all the 'what ifs.'

"It's not just about wanting to help the neighbors. If the kids find out, they'll be all over us to move. Milt, I really don't want to move. I like it here."

"I like it here too. But let's not get ahead of ourselves. Let's wait for more information, then we'll decide what needs to be done."

I stopped pacing and looked at him. Milt might not want to get ahead of himself, but I had no problem doing that. "Do you have Sol's office number somewhere? You called him a few years ago about something. Did you save his number?"

"What are you up to?" Milt's tone took on an edge.

"What do you mean, what am I up to? I want to call Sol and tell him how upsetting this is to the tenants. I want him to come here and talk to us. I want some answers. What I don't want is to sit back and do nothing."

"I didn't suggest we do nothing," Milt argued. "I said we should wait for more information."

"I have no problem with the information part, it's the waiting part I don't like."

"Oh come on Sadie. This is a business situation. You might not like it, we might not like it, but sometimes things are out of our hands."

"If the building gets sold, it gets sold. However, I can't accept the 'out of our hands' part without getting involved. I'm not saying I'm going to change Sol's mind or make a huge difference, but I do want to let him know how his decision affects the tenants. Maybe there's another way of going about selling the place."

Milt's look told me he wasn't happy with my little speech, but to his credit, he didn't belabor the issue. Without another word, he turned, went to his desk and rummaged through his drawer. Moments later he handed me Sol's business card. In spite of my frustration with Milt's resistance, I had to admire his organizational abilities. The man could probably locate the first bill he ever paid.

"Thanks," I said, offering a conciliatory smile. "I'll call him right now."

"If you insist on calling, try not to fire all your missiles at once," Milt called out as I walked into the kitchen to use the phone. "At least give him a chance to explain."

I got through to Sol's secretary who informed me in a tight, formal tone, that her boss was not in, nor was he expected back until later that morning. I left a message, identifying myself as one of his tenants, and asked that he call me as soon as he returned.

If I am anything, I'm tenacious. I don't like loose ends or unresolved situations. I waited 15 minutes and called again, getting the same response.

The secretary, sounding very much annoyed, tried to persuade me not to continue calling. "He's not here," she said testily. "I'll pass along the message that you called." She hung up.

Of course I called again. This time I got lucky. Ms. Secretary must have left her desk for a moment. The phone rang several times before it was picked up. A male voice yelled into the receiver, "Rubenstein Properties."

"Sol Rubenstein?"

"Yeah, who's this?"

"This is Sonja Maven from apartment 4-C in your building. The neighbors, uh, well, we, I mean, I read your notice about the sale and it's terrible that you're doing this. You shouldn't. The tenants are old, they have rent control and now they won't be able to move anywhere else because of the expense. Even my husband and I don't want to move because we like it here." Having run out of breath, I stopped babbling, which I tend to do when I'm nervous, excited, or have consumed too much caffeine.

"Who's this again?"

"Sonja Maven from…"

"Yeah, okay. Look, it's a business deal, plain and simple. I'm sorry the tenants are upset. That's not my intention, but you know, the market's good now and I found buyers who are offering a great price."

"Mr. Rubenstein, I understand this is a business deal, but your father lives in the building too. Look at the inconvenience it will cause him while the building's being renovated, unless of course, you're planning to move him in with you." I let my words sink in for a moment.

I'd been told that Sol's second wife, Sabrina, a former Las Vegas showgirl, was hostile to Sol's father, so the likelihood of Sol having his father live with them was highly unlikely.

"Maybe there's a way to do the conversion gradually," I continued. "One or two apartments at a time so not all the tenants are displaced at once. Give some of the older folks time to adjust and make other plans."

"Mrs. Maven," he said firmly. "The place is being sold in thirty days. After inspections and some legal stuff, the property officially belongs to the buyers. I can't tell them what to do with it once the papers are signed."

"I'm not saying you should tell anyone what to do. Actually, I'm calling to invite you to come and talk to us. It might defuse some of the tension and hostility here."

"Tension and hostility? You make it sound like a war zone."

"In a way it is. That's why it's important for you to talk to the tenants. They have a lot of questions."

"Well…I don't see why this is such a big deal, but, oh what the hell. I was planning to stop by to see my father this evening anyway. I'll make a quick five, ten minute appearance, but I don't want a bunch of angry people challenging my business decisions."

"Mr. Rubenstein, the tenants are angry. That's not going change just because you want it to."

"Then why should I even bother talking to them?" He demanded.

"Because, at the very least, it might make them feel better."

"Yeah, all right, whatever." He voice was tight. "I suppose I could be there around seven."

I began to thank him but he had already hung up.

"He agreed to come?" Milt stood by the kitchen door. "I'm surprised. I'd think that meeting with the very tenants he's displacing would be the last thing he'd want to do."

"Well, he didn't exactly want to do this," I said, surprised that Milt was interested in the call. "Maybe he agreed to come here out of respect for his father, or maybe he's not exactly the monster everyone is making him out to be."

Milt started to say something, then for whatever reason decided not to. He nodded and went back into the living room.

Figuring it best to give Milt his space rather than continue with this discussion, I hastily made a notice announcing the seven o'clock meeting. I yelled a quick, 'be right back' to Milt. Then, wanting a little exercise, took the stairs down to the lobby where I placed the flyer on the wall next to the 'property to be sold' announcement.

I was nervous and out of sorts, glad Sol was coming, yet apprehensive about the reaction he might receive. I went back up in the elevator this time and knocked on Mrs. Pinsky's door. She opened the door, wringing her hands, repeating "oy, oy" over and over as she paced back and forth. Still clearly distraught by the news of the pending sale, I tried to calm her down. I told her about Sol agreeing to the meeting that evening which seemed to help her anxiety. When I put her in charge of 'spreading the word' to the neighbors she actually smiled.

"This is good. We need to unite! We need to stand together," she said, raising her hands in what looked like an age appropriate victory salute of sorts.

Satisfied that she would be okay with her designated mission, I spent the rest of the day answering phone calls and talking to neighbors who dropped by to ask if I'd heard anything new, if the meeting was still on for that evening, or if I felt there was a chance that the building wouldn't be sold after all. I didn't have any answers except to confirm that, as far as I knew, the meeting was still on.

By five o'clock Milt said he was hungry. We hadn't spoken more than a few words since my phone call to Sol. I knew he was annoyed with me but I hoped sitting across from each other over dinner would break the stalemate between us.

I went into the kitchen to take an inventory of my refrigerator. I'm big on leftovers, so between three cartons of frozen Chinese food and salad stuff that hadn't turned brown yet, we managed to eat a reasonably good dinner. It wasn't gourmet, but it worked. I even found two fortune cookies to go with the mint chocolate chip ice cream I served for dessert.

Milt held the cookies out to me. I selected a cookie, hoping for a fortune that would predict an optimistic outcome to the day's events. "'You will have a memorable week of personal intrigue,'" I read. "Personal intrigue? What does that mean?"

"I have no idea." Milt reached for the remaining cookie. "'Your patience initially will be highly tested.'" We looked at each other, slightly uncomfortable with the too-close-for-comfort truth of the message. "Who writes these things?"

"Beats me," I said. "Makes you wonder what ever happened to fortunes by Confucius."

After clearing the table, I was ready to get Mrs. Pinsky and head down to the meeting. Milt was making a statement by not going. "Sol's not going to give out details on the sale until it goes through," he had said earlier. "The meeting will stir things up and get everyone mad."

I could have insisted he come with me. I could have tried to reason with him, but after forty-plus years of marriage, we both knew when to push and when to let go. This was not worth fighting over. I kissed him good bye and told him I'd fill him in when I got back.

Mrs. Pinsky was waiting outside her door as I approached. "I'm glad there's a meeting. I hope Sol comes to his senses and sees what this sale is doing to us."

"Please, Mrs. Pinsky, don't get yourself all worked up again."

"Worked up? How can I not get worked up? This is affecting our lives. All the neighbors I spoke to are worked up. They're angry, confused, afraid. They want to know if he'll give us time to make other arrangements or offer help finding other housing."

"I understand and I agree. But I don't know any more than you do at this point, although I did ask if he planned on having his father move in with him. I don't think he appreciated that question."

"I'm not surprised." Mrs. Pinsky snorted, her attempt at a chuckle. "Sabrina wouldn't last five minutes in the same room with her father-in-law. My friend Mrs. Cohen, lives next door to Sol's father. She says she hears arguing as soon as Sabrina and Sol walk in to the apartment. Sabrina yells at Sol to hurry up and finish his business with his father so they can leave. Mrs. Cohen assures me she's not eavesdropping. She says the conversation is so loud she can't avoid hearing everything."

As we exited the elevator, Mrs. Pinsky whispered. "Of course if I know Mrs. Cohen, she probably keeps a glass near the connecting wall."

Another snort from my friend Mrs. Pinsky!

CHAPTER TWO

The meeting was in the lobby where Sol Rubenstein had apparently arranged to have folding chairs set up. A crowd had already gathered when Mrs. Pinsky and I walked in a few minutes after seven. Sol had not arrived and from the noise level I knew the natives were getting restless.

Twenty minutes later Sol walked in accompanied by Sabrina and two men, a short, beefy guy in his early twenties and a tall, buff guy, slightly older. I couldn't figure out if they were Sol's assistants, bodyguards or both.

"He's the one I saw hanging up the notice this morning," she said, pointing to the taller man.

I nodded, distracted by Sol's wife as she walked by. Close to thirty, Sabrina was a knockout with long blond hair and a Las Vegas body. Taller than Sol by at least three inches, she stood quietly next to her husband, her eyes staring blankly at some distant space.

My attention moved from Sabrina to the two men standing with Sol. The taller one, well over six feet and heavy set, was wearing the strangest pair of shoes I had ever seen. Loafers in an odd combination of green and what looked to me like dark purple. Micro lights, like kids sometimes wear in their sneakers, were embedded in the side of each shoe, lighting up when moved. In spite of the serious nature of the meeting, I was momentarily mesmerized by the sheer outrageousness of the shoes.

The other man was probably five eight or five nine and extremely muscular. He was chewing gum, open mouth, non stop. I was tempted to run up to him and tell him to get rid of the gum, but reason prevailed and I didn't. As I stared at him, he placed a small step stool, which he had carried in with him, on the floor. Sol, dressed in a dark suit, white shirt and tie, stepped up and raised his hands. The room quieted.

At fifty-two, Sol wore thick glasses, was nearly bald, quite short and seriously over weight. In a strong, no nonsense voice, he told us that the selling of the building was a business deal and that after a mandatory thirty-day period, it would be a *fait accompli.*

"Thirty days isn't giving most of us enough time to make other housing arrangements," Mrs. Watkins, a widow in 5-B, bellowed across the room. "Is there any chance the sale might not go through?"

"No." Sol answered. "Any other questions?"

"You're not being fair to the tenants," 2-D chimed in.

"We could take you to court," 6-F added, pushing his way to the front of the room.

"Look folks," Sol said, clearly impatient. "This is a legal business transaction. You want to take me to court, go ahead, but I'm telling you, there are lawyers on both sides of the table looking this over and I assure you it is legal. Once it's signed, it's binding. Now, if there are no further questions, I have to go."

"Excuse me, Mr. Rubenstein," I called out, surprised at the lack of compassion Sol showed for his tenants. "Isn't there anything you could do to help us? You're in property management. Couldn't you provide lists of available and affordable housing in the area, or names and telephone numbers of places that have that information?"

"Sure, sure," Sol replied with an air of indifference. "I'll take care of it tomorrow." He looked around the room, apparently eager to step down from his little platform and make a speedy exit.

"Wait a minute. Not so fast." John Brunner, from apartment 6-C, yelled. "What the hell are we supposed to do now?" John was standing next to his wife, Helen, the woman who had snubbed me earlier. "We've paid our rent here on time for six years. We can't afford fancy condo prices. You'll be forcing me and my wife out on the street along with all the other tenants. What do you have to say about that?" A former Marine, John was shaking his fist at Sol and turning red in the process.

"I understand your reaction," Sol answered with that same air of indifference. "Perhaps you could take up your concerns with the new owners once they take over the property. Now, I have to leave. I have another appointment." Sol stepped down, turned and started to walk out of the room, followed by Sabrina and the two men.

"That's it?" John continued yelling. "No remorse? No compassion? Maybe you need a wake up call. Maybe a little push to help you see it from our side. Huh?"

Sol's cavalier reaction as he continued to walk away ignited more angry shouting and waving fists. To me, the sound was like road rage without the road. My mind started imagining all kinds of scenarios, a flash of gun, a mob advancing on Sol and his entourage, or a fist fight out of control.

"You're just a greedy, heartless, businessman, aren't you?" Chuck Dudley called out. He and his younger brother, Pete, lived on the second floor. Both in their twenties, they kept pretty much to themselves, giving us little if any information about who they were, what they did, or where they were from.

"What about the older people who live here?" Chuck continued, clearly agitated. "What are they supposed to do? You only care about the almighty dollar." His hands were balled into fists. Suddenly he grabbed Pete, propelling him forward towards the front of the room.

Both Sol's men and I tensed. "Uh, oh," I said to Mrs. Pinsky, "this is getting ugly."

Sol's men stepped in front of Chuck and Pete, blocking their path. The four glared at each other, daring the other guy to make the first move. Quickly, Pete whispered something to Chuck. They turned abruptly and left, leaving the rest of us wondering what that had been about.

Once the Dudley brothers left, much of the tension subsided. Sol and Sabrina walked out with their entourage, followed minutes later by Helen and John Brunner. Other tenants, still agitated at the outcome of the meeting, began making their way out of the room as well.

I took a deep breath, grateful that nothing worse had happened.

Mrs. Pinsky and I were quiet as we joined a group of tenants walking towards the elevator.

"So what does all this mean, Mrs. Maven?" Mrs. Pinsky sighed deeply as she walked slowly along side me. The steam had gone out of her fire. "It's over, isn't it? This building, our apartment. We're going to have to move now, right?"

"I'm afraid so, Mrs. Pinsky." For a moment I was as devastated as she was. I'd hoped Sol would offer a few words of support or assistance, maybe even initiate a hot line to his office. Milt had been right. Sol had not given us any more details on the sale, and the meeting had just riled the tenants up and made everyone mad.

I didn't like this feeling of helplessness. This was not my style.

"You know what? I'm not going to give up and neither should you Mrs. Pinsky. Give me a couple of days to see what I can do. Maybe I'll find out who the new owners are and talk to them." I thought it unlikely that I'd be able to change anyone's mind, but it seemed worth a try.

I pressed the elevator button, feeling energized again. "Worst case, if we have to move, we'll move. You have your family. Milt and I will find a place near, but not too near our children and we'll make it work. As for some of the older tenants who have no other place to go, well, I'll check online and see what resources are available. Maybe I'll organize a group of volunteers to help find alternative housing."

Who knew? At the time I really believed I might be able to make a difference. At the very least, I felt prepared to give it my best shot.

CHAPTER THREE

Milt was on the couch when I walked in. He was in his pajamas and robe, watching a basketball game.

"Are you okay?" I was surprised to see him bundled up like that.

"I think I'm coming down with a cold. My throat's scratchy and I'm chilled. How come you're back so soon anyway? That was a quick meeting."

"It was ugly." I felt his forehead. "You're warm. You should get into bed."

"Yeah, I will. I want to see the end of the game."

"I'll make you tea." I went into the kitchen. "You were right about the meeting. Sol made it absolutely clear that the sale will take place, and that it was final. He couldn't wait to leave. Even his bodyguards looked spooked by the crowd."

"What a shot!" Milt yelled from the other room, totally immersed in the game.

I rolled my eyes, smiling at Milt's unabashed enthusiasm for the game.

"Sadie," he called out, a few seconds later.

"Yes?" I poured tea into a large mug.

"Don't take this Sol business too seriously. Everything will work out. You'll see."

It had to be a commercial break. I knew Milt's comment was an attempt to show interest and to make up for his edgy response earlier. He meant well, but telling me not to take it so seriously, uh uh. That was not going to happen.

I gave Milt his tea. Then I went to my desk in the second bedroom where I had my computer. I went online, checking alternative housing. I found everything from modular housing to rentals, sublets and foreclosures. Before I could dig deeper, I was distracted by the sounds of approaching sirens. Sirens, like burglaries, were not uncommon in Brooklyn, so most of the time I didn't pay too much attention. This, however, was different. The sirens were loud and getting closer. I went to the big window in our living room. It faced the street, giving me a clear view of the front of our building.

"Milt, police cars are stopping here, right in front! I have a bad feeling about this." I grabbed my sweater from the hall closest. "I'm going to check it out."

"Do you want me to come with you?"

"No. Stay and keep warm. There's no need for both of us to go."

Not wanting to wait for the elevator, I headed to the stairs. Besides providing a little exercise for me every now and then, I liked the openness of the stairway. You could see all the way down to the bottom floor, or all the way up to the top.

Working my way down, I saw several distraught looking tenants clustered near the base of the stairs. Paramedics and two men, wearing sport jackets, shirts and loosened ties, stood around something or, oh my, someone now covered in a sheet laying on the ground in the center of the stairwell.

One of the men walked over to me as I reached the bottom step. He was close to five ten or eleven and looked to be in his late thirties. He seemed familiar. I tried to place him, when suddenly surprise registered in his face as he apparently recognized me.

"Mrs. Maven, right? I remember you." His voice was strong and commanding. "I'm Andy Cohen." He gave me a tentative hug.

"Andy? Andy Cohen?" I blurted out. "My goodness, I haven't seen you since you were a kid in my Sunday school class. Are you with the police? What's going on?"

"I'm a detective in the homicide division. My partner," he pointed to a tall, nice-looking man talking to one of the paramedics, "is Brian Masters. How've you been?"

"Fine, fine. How's your mother?" I was so shocked to see my former student, I forgot for a moment about the body lying practically at my feet.

Just then his partner approached. He coughed, bringing us back to reality.

"Andy, what happened here?" I asked. "Who's under the sheet?" I held my breath, fearing it might be Mrs. Pinsky, or any one of the older tenants in the building.

Andy looked at his partner, gave a nod and gently took my arm, leading me away from the body. "According to the identification we found on the body, his name's Sol Rubenstein. Does that mean anything to you?"

"Sol Rubenstein? He's dead? How? When?" My heart felt as though it had dropped down to my stomach.

"That's what we're trying to find out. You know him?"

"Well, yes. He's our landlord. His father...oh my." My hand flew to my mouth. I looked around nervously.

"What about his father?" Andy asked, studying my reaction.

"His father, Morris Rubenstein, lives in 1-F. He's in his eighties. I was looking to see if he's here. I wouldn't want him to find out about his son like this."

Matt was taking notes. "Does his son live with him?"

"No, no, not at all. Sol visits his father from time to time, but no, he was here because, oh my..." I let out a big sigh. "You see, Sol announced he was selling the building. That's why he was here, to talk to the tenants about the sale. The new owners, once the sale goes through, will turn the apartments into condos. Many of the tenants have rent control which would end with the sale. And several don't have anywhere else to go." I exhaled. I was babbling again. My words were spilling out so fast I wondered if I was making any sense.

"How'd the meeting go?" Andy asked patiently.

"Not very well, I'm afraid." I closed my eyes, visualizing the meeting. "There were a lot of angry people there."

"Any one become violent, or threatening?"

I hesitated, uncomfortable naming names.

"Mrs. Maven, if you know anything that might help us, you need to tell me now." Andy looked directly at me, staring until I nodded.

"Well, no one was actually violent, although several people were loud and seemed on the verge of getting to that point," I explained.

"What do you mean, on the verge?" Andy questioned.

"A few had their fists raised. There were two guys, brothers actually, who ran up to Sol and, for a moment, I was sure there would be a fist fight."

"Was there?"

"No. It was like a fire cracker that just fizzles out. There was a standoff between the two brothers, Sol and the two men with him. Then it was over."

"Just like that? What happened?"

"Honestly," I said. "I don't know. They walked out."

"Walked out?" Andy looked puzzled. "That was it?"

"Yes. Sol had showed up late. He came with his wife and two men, bodyguards I think. He made a brief announcement confirming the sale. Several tenants yelled at Sol, there was the confrontation with the brothers, then Sol and his group left. After that, the rest of us, still angry at Sol's cavalier attitude and the hostility in the room, left as well."

I watched Andy write in his notebook. "I don't understand, Andy. Why all these questions about threats and violence? Surely you don't think his death had anything to do with the meeting or the tenants? Sol's death was probably from a heart attack or maybe he tripped and hit his head, right?"

"I'm sorry." He said sympathetically. "We'll need a coroner's official ruling, but from the position of the body, we definitely suspect foul play."

"Foul play? You mean like murder?"

"I'm afraid so. It looks like he fell or was pushed over the railing from one of the upper floors."

Andy's words hit me hard. I didn't consider myself naïve. I knew bad things happened. But even with the threats at the meeting, I couldn't connect any of that to murder.

I felt the color drain from my face. I must have staggered slightly, because Andy, probably concerned that he might have another body to contend with, grabbed my arm.

"Are you all right? Do you want to sit down?" He walked me towards the steps.

"No. I'm fine. I'm just, I don't know, bewildered, sad, shocked, take your pick." I took a deep breath. "You really think he was killed by someone at the meeting?"

"Right now we don't know who killed him. That's why I need you to tell me everything you can remember about the evening."

"But I've told you everything, Andy."

"Let's go over it again anyway. Something might jump out at you. Who were the neighbors you heard making threatening remarks?"

Reluctantly I described in more detail John Brunner's outburst and the Dudley brothers' explosive behavior.

"Andy," I said when I was through, "can I ask you a question?"

"Okay," He answered with a slight hesitation.

"How did the police know to come here?"

"We got a call at 9:35 p.m. from that man over there, Alan Pacey." He pointed to a slender man talking to a policewoman. "Mr. Pacey told us that he and his family were walking in when they saw the body. He told his wife to take the children upstairs and to call 911, which she did. Now, Mrs. Maven," Andy said, reaching into his pocket for his business card. "I've got to get back to work. Thanks for your help. Don't hesitate to call me if you think of anything else, no matter how trivial it might sound to you. Okay?"

I took the card and nodded. Andy turned and headed to his partner.

I didn't know how I made it back to my apartment. I had no memory of walking to the elevator or riding up to my floor. In a daze, I replayed the scene at the meeting, the threats and all that anger in the room with no outlet or resolve. I wasn't used to any of this negative energy, let alone murder. I was a grandmother, for goodness sakes. Grandmothers don't get themselves involved in murders. Okay, so maybe Sol wasn't the nicest person in the world. Maybe he was selfish, selling the property to make a profit. That didn't mean he deserved to be murdered. He was someone's son, someone's husband and, for better or for worse, he was a human being.

I pictured Sol Rubenstein dead under that sheet. Murdered. Oh my God, how awful. I buried my face in my hands and cried!

CHAPTER FOUR

I was a wreck when I returned to our apartment. I found Milt in bed, propped up with a couple of pillows, reviewing income tax forms.

I probably should have asked Milt how he was feeling or if he needed anything, but I didn't. I barged right in with all the details of finding the body, discovering it was Sol's, stumbling into Andy, and how I gave out details that could possibly implicate a few of the neighbors.

"Sadie, Sadie, calm down, take a breath." Milt reached out and took my hand.

"Milt, Sol was murdered," I repeated. "Right here in this building. Oh, this is my fault. If I hadn't asked him to come here tonight, this wouldn't have happened."

"Whoa. Hold on there. This is a terrible thing, but it is absolutely not your fault. You didn't kill him. If this was a murder, then whoever wanted him dead would have found a way to kill him, with or without your help, here or somewhere else."

I took a few more deep breaths. "I don't know, Milt. I feel very guilty about the whole thing. I mean, if he wasn't here, he wouldn't be dead now, period."

"I'm not so sure about that." Milt got out of bed and followed me into the kitchen. "Either way you can't blame yourself for this. Look, I didn't agree with what you were doing, but to be fair, you were trying to help the neighbors by reaching out to both sides. I'm proud of you for that. You shouldn't feel guilty about any of this."

"Thanks for your vote of confidence." I said meekly, giving Milt a hug and feeling grateful for his understanding. "Oh, you still feel warm. You should get back in bed. I'm sorry I disturbed you with this."

"It's okay. I'll be fine, it's just a little cold, if that. Maybe it's my allergies starting early this year. Meanwhile, don't add any more guilt, Sadie. Your plate's already pretty full."

"Speaking of guilt," I said. "I told Andy about John Brunner and the Dudley brothers threatening tone and angry comments. Now the police are focusing on them. But suppose it had nothing to do with the neighbors, or even that the building was going to be sold? After all, Sol was a business man. Maybe it was a deal that didn't go well."

"Could be," Milt sat down at the kitchen table. "But here's an idea. Why not let the police work it out? I'm sure they'll call you if they need your help."

"Hey," I said, a bit miffed at his sarcasm. "That's not nice."

"Sorry," Milt held up his hands in mock defeat. "I couldn't resist. You can't help yourself. You have to get personally involved in every little thing that happens around here."

"Little thing? Milt," I said, getting ready to jump on my soap box. "Murder is not a 'little thing' and, if getting involved means helping people when they are in trouble and making a difference, then I stand by my actions proudly."

"Okay, okay, I give up," Milt said. "I'm going back to bed."

I didn't argue. I still had guilt feelings about Sol's murder and would have been extra sensitive to whatever Milt said. Convincing myself that Milt was better off in a warm bed instead of standing in the kitchen debating with me, I went to the cabinet drawer, found a pencil and pad of paper, and began jotting down thoughts as they popped in my head.

"Now that I think of it," I said, finding it helpful to talk to myself as I tried to figure things out, "the two men who came in with Sol and Sabrina could have had something to do with the murder. I should have mentioned this to Andy. I wonder who hired them? Maybe they were professional killers."

I wrote bodyguards/assistants, with a question mark, since I wasn't sure which they were. I added a note to ask Andy about Sabrina too, wondering if she would benefit financially from her husband's death. Without realizing it, I'd gone from dazed, guilt-ridden mode to curious, determined to take-charge mode. Apparently I was so absorbed in my own ruminating, I didn't hear Milt walk back into the room.

"Honey. What are you doing?" Milt asked, catching me off guard.

"Doing?" I looked up at Milt's quizzical look. "What do you mean? I'm just thinking out loud about the murder. Why, what's the matter?"

"I'm worried, that's what." Milt looked at the notes I had written.

27

"Worried? About what?" I had no clue where this was going.

"I don't want you to G.P.I.!" Milt said, looking very serious.

"What? Milt. What in the world is G.P.I.?"

"Get Permanently Involved!" Milt actually smiled. "I know you, Sadie. You're not going to be content to just make a few phone calls or offer to help out a little. You're going to jump right into the middle of everyone's business and become practically insane. You'll talk of nothing else and get yourself all wound up, just like you are right now."

"You're right. But I'm sorry, I'm not about to sit back and do nothing. And besides, I feel responsible, even if only partially. I'm going to do everything I can to help the police find the person who killed Sol."

"Sadie," Milt spoke slowly, as if to a child. "This is murder we're talking about. You have got to let the police handle it. Please, I'm serious about this."

"I know, I know." I said, trying to reassure him. "Don't worry so much. I'm not going to join a posse. I'm just writing down some thoughts to discuss with Andy. To help. That's all."

"That's all?" Milt scratched his head. "If I could believe that, I'd feel a lot better. Somehow I can't see you stopping at just writing down thoughts."

"What do you think I'm going to do, Milt? Come on, you're not being fair."

"I'm not being fair? And you butting in on a police investigation is your idea of fair?"

Oh boy, this was not going well.

"Milt, let's not get ourselves out of control over this. I'm just writing down a few questions I want to talk to Andy about. Okay?"

"Okay. Fine." Milt walked back to the bedroom.

Wow. I massaged my temples. I'd have to be very careful if I wanted to avoid any more exchanges like this. I looked to make sure that Milt had returned to bed.

Then I turned to my notes, adding my thoughts as I spoke them softly to myself. "I need to find out how Sol's death affects the pending sale. I'd love to get Sabrina talking to me, but that was unlikely, given her unapproachable attitude and demeanor. I should also talk to Sol's father, offer condolences, see if he needs anything."

I sat, I wrote, I stood, I paced.

"Come to bed, Sadie," Milt called from the bedroom an hour later. "Enough with the Sherlock Holmes already."

To keep the peace, I finally did go to bed, but I couldn't fall asleep. My mind was on full throttle, energized with enough questions to keep me awake for the better part of the night. Maybe a little private investigating on my part wouldn't be such a bad idea. Maybe, I'd even turn up something useful.

If I'd known that evening the trouble I'd be getting myself into, I might have taken Milt's advice and gone off to sleep without another thought of becoming personally involved.

But of course I didn't. I waited until Milt was in a deep sleep, snoring loudly. I quietly slid out from under the covers, grabbed my robe, and went into the kitchen. I boiled some water for tea, found my note-pad, and continued writing down my thoughts.

In addition to the neighbors who had made threats or accusations at the meeting, I listed those tenants who had the most to lose when the building sold, no family, no income, and no place to go.

Then I outlined questions, including where the two assistants, a.k.a bodyguards, were when Sol was murdered; if Sol was indeed thrown over the railing, what floor was he on and what was he doing there; and where was Sabrina during all this, since she had been with him during the meeting and was still there when I had left. I also wanted to find out if Sol went to his father's apartment before or after the meeting.

Andy had told me that he was going to be talking to the neighbors, so I assumed he'd be asking many of these same questions. Since I knew many of my neighbors, I felt that gave me an edge. I was counting on them opening up more to me than they would to the police.

I finished my tea, gathered up my papers and quietly went to my desk and computer in the second bedroom. I placed my notes in a drawer intending to create a 'Sol Rubenstein' computer file first thing in the morning when Milt would be working on our taxes.

I returned to bed, careful not to disturb Milt. Eventually I fell asleep, although, for most of the night I tossed and turned, moving between deep sleep and dreams that were fitful and upsetting.

I dreamt of being chased, of dark storm clouds and of being locked in a place I couldn't identify. I woke up sweating, despite the early morning chill in the room. If I'd taken the time to analyze the meaning of my dreams, I'd have been forewarned of what lay ahead, a journey froth with turbulence, evil and extreme danger.

CHAPTER FIVE

I woke up early the next day and took a hot shower to shake off the sweats and malaise. By 8:15 I was dressed and in the kitchen. Milt walked in, yawning and stretching at the same time. I didn't tell him about my nocturnal musings, thankful that he had not heard me get up from bed after he had fallen asleep.

"Feeling better?" I poured us both a cup of coffee.

"Actually I do," he said, taking a sip. "My throat doesn't hurt as much, although I'm still a little congested."

The ringing of the phone made us both jump.

"Hi Mom. Hope I'm not calling too early." Our daughter's voice caught me off guard.

"Frannie? What's the matter? Everyone okay?" Early morning calls from my children were not a typical occurrence.

"Yes, Mom. We're okay. Why do you always assume something bad has happened when I call?"

"Sorry. It's a bad habit. I do the same when your brother calls."

"Yes, so I've been told. Look. Everything is fine. It's just that I heard about the murder, so I thought if you and Dad were going to be home, Julie and I would drive out for a visit some time around noon. We haven't seen you for a while and this would a good opportunity if it fit in with your plans.

"Well sure, we'd love to see you and Julie, but I hope you're not overly upset or concerned. The murder was certainly an awful thing to have happened, but Dad and I are fine."

"No." I heard the hesitation in her voice. "Not overly concerned. I do want to ask you about it though, especially since it happened right in the building. It must have been awful. I'd feel better if I could see you and get the full story. I'll stop at the deli on the way over, so don't fuss with anything for lunch."

"That would be nice." I hoped my voice didn't betray my feelings. While I understood her concern and knew she needed to see for herself that we were okay, the timing was bad. I had been planning to spend the day working on the computer, making calls and talking to the neighbors about Sol's murder. Now I'd have to condense it into the few hours before and after their visit.

After we hung up I checked with Milt to make sure he felt up to their visit.

"I'm fine," he assured me. "Whatever I had seems to have passed. I'm not even as congested as I was before. You know I wouldn't take any chances around the kids."

I nodded. "Just checking to make sure."

After straightening up the apartment I called Andy, using the number he'd given me on his card. I knew he wouldn't talk about the case, however I was hoping our previous 'favorite teacher-student relationship' would get me a few tidbits of information. He was out. I left a message for him to call when he returned.

I went next door to Mrs. Pinsky. I was wondering if she knew about Sol's murder yet, although very few things ever got by her. I knocked on her door. When there was no answer I became concerned, until I remembered that she'd told me she had a doctor's appointment.

I returned to our apartment, glad to see Milt distracted with the tax forms he had spread out on the kitchen table. If Milt was uncomfortable with my particular interest in Sol's murder, it would be a lot better for both of us if he didn't see any of my actual activities and potential involvement.

After calling out a quick, "hello" to Milt, I retreated to my desk to review the notes I'd scribbled the night before. I tried Andy's number again and left a second message.

Just before noon, our daughter and granddaughter arrived.

Amidst a jumble of hugs and kisses at the door, Julie handed us a large bouquet of spring flowers.

"She picked these out all by herself," Frannie explained as Julie danced around Milt and me.

"Julie, the flowers are lovely," Milt complimented our granddaughter.

"Yes, they sure are," I agreed. "You did a great job picking out the nicest color combination. They look lovely on the table, too." I bent down and gave her a hug.

"Julie," Frannie said as she placed the deli bag in the refrigerator, "why don't you go set up your toys in the living room. Mommy wants to talk to Grandma and Papa in the kitchen. Okay?"

When Julie did as she was instructed, our daughter immediately unleashed a barrage of questions that had apparently been bothering her since hearing about the murder.

"What's the scoop? Do the police have any motive for the killing? Was it for the money? Do they know who did it?"

"Bottom line," Milt told her, "we don't know. Your mother has a relationship with the detective investigating the murder, but so far, at least, he hasn't confided in her," Milt added with a chuckle.

"What do you mean, relationship?" She looked at us both.

"Do you remember Andy Cohen from religious school?" I asked, trying to take back the conversation. Milt thought his comments were funny. I didn't, but I chose not to get into a war of words with him in front of Frannie.

"Actually I believe he's close to your age, although he might have been a year ahead of you." I continued. "Well, he's now a Homicide Detective."

"The name sounds familiar. But what did Dad mean, that he hasn't confided in you yet? Mom, you don't seriously expect to be kept in the loop just because he was your student when he was nine or ten years old. Do you?"

"Don't be silly Frannie. Dad was kidding. I just found it interesting to run into Andy, even though the circumstances were awful."

"You know what, Mom, Dad? I'm not comfortable with what's going on here." Frannie suddenly stood up and began pacing in front of us. "It could be some crazy serial killer. You could be his next target. What about your door locks, how secure are they by the way? You know how easy it is for people to get through even the strongest locks these days? I'd feel a lot better if you came out and stayed with us. At least until they catch the killer. Let the police do their thing. Besides, it's time you gave some serious consideration to moving out to us. This would be a perfect opportunity to scope out the communities to see what you like."

This was the last thing I wanted to do.

Milt and I exchanged looks.

"Grandma and Papa coming to my house?" Julie asked as she ran into the kitchen. "Yay! Grandma and Papa are coming to my house. Yay!"

"Thank you Frannie, and Julie for your invitation, but no, I'm afraid we can't come right now," I said as patiently as I could. "It could take weeks before the police catch the person who did this. We can't be away that long. We have appointments, obligations. We can't just pick up and leave like that."

"What your mother means," Milt said with a straight face, "is that she wants to solve the murder all by herself and she couldn't possibly do that if she wasn't right here in the middle of it all."

I gave Milt a hard look. I didn't appreciate being teased about this.

"No, that's not what I'm saying Milt. Don't you agree that it wouldn't be a good idea to be away right now?" I reasoned. "I mean, after all, you have all the tax forms to complete and you have a meeting with the accountant. And for me, well, between my volunteer commitments, my book group, exercise class, and grocery shopping, not to mention all the other little things I do on a day to day basis, I'm just not ready to get up and leave so fast."

"Okay, okay, you're right." Milt said, pursing his lips tightly.

"Come on Mom," Frannie said. "This is really serious stuff and I'm worried about you becoming way too involved in the investigation."

"You tell her Frannie." Milt said. "I can't seem to get through to her. Your mother's made a list of people she's going to interview, questions she wants to ask them and basically doing the work she should be leaving to the police."

"Milt, that's not fair." I started to protest again, but Frannie interrupted.

"I don't like this. Look what's happening between you and Dad. He's upset and you're defensive. Bottom line, you shouldn't be interfering. Period! I know you mean well, but looking for a murderer is a lot different than looking for a toy stuck in someone's bathtub, or finding a neighbor the name of a good orthopedic surgeon. Promise me you're not going to continue doing this. I'm nervous enough about what happened here. I don't need to be worrying about you coming up against a killer."

Oh brother! Things were getting way out of control and I was not happy about that at all. Their loud voices were also upsetting Julie, who was now giving us a puzzled look.

"See what you started Milt?" I was trying unsuccessfully to direct some guilt his way.

I turned to my daughter. "Come on Frannie. It's going to be okay," "Don't worry. I'm not going to do anything rash or stupid. I'm going to ask a few questions here and there, that's all."

Frannie rolled her eyes, looking imploringly at her father. But before either of them could counter with a logical rebuttal, Julie came to my rescue.

"I'm hungry."

Ah, thank goodness for Julie.

Frannie and I got up, took out the containers of deli foods, and placed everything on the table. We ate in silence, even Julie, who was normally very animated. Either we were all very hungry, or very deep in thought.

"Grandma, I'm done. Come play with me." Julie pushed her plate away.

So I did, grateful to leave the table. Milt and Frannie cleared as I followed Julie into the living room. I was certain they were going to talk about me and my investigating activities, but I was determined not to let that bother me.

As Julie and I sat on the living room floor among Barbie and her paraphernalia, I thought of how many times over the years I'd sat with a grandchild, playing with dolls or trucks, or Legos, Chutes and Ladders, and Candy Land. I let my mind wander, feeling at peace for the first time since finding that pending sale notice Wednesday morning.

"Grandma," she scolded. "You're not paying attention. You're supposed to get Barbie dressed for the ice-skating party."

Properly admonished, I returned to my assigned duties, dressing Barbie in an ice skating outfit appropriately befitting a beauty queen.

By two-thirty, Frannie and Julie were getting ready to leave.

"You promise you'll call if anything happens?" Frannie looked at both of us.

"Yes, I promise." I gave her a hug. "Please don't worry. I'm not in any danger and we'll keep you posted on all the latest developments as they unfold. Okay?"

"I do worry, Mom. I'm very uneasy about the murder and your personal interest in it."

"I understand how you feel, but really, lighten up a bit. I'm not exactly going into a war zone."

"Okay," she said softly. "I guess I'm overreacting, but I do worry about you. I come by that naturally, by the way."

"I know. I know," I said, giving her an extra tight squeeze.

Milt and I took the elevator down with them. We walked the short distance to their car, gave another round of hugs and kisses, then waved as they drove off.

When we returned to the apartment, I grabbed my keys.

"Where are you going now?" Milt asked.

"I'm going to visit a few of the neighbors," I answered abruptly, still miffed.

"Didn't you just assure our daughter that you weren't going to get personally involved? Why don't you just let the police handle this, for goodness sakes. It's way out of your league."

"Milt," I said firmly. "I never promised Frannie, or anyone else for that matter, that I wouldn't get involved. I promised to call her if anything happens, that's all. As for getting involved, like it or not, I am

39

involved. The murder happened here, in this building, and that affects us all."

"Yes, it affects us all," Milt said. "But that doesn't mean we all have to go traipsing around, knocking on doors, asking questions and driving everyone crazy."

"Look," I said patiently, hoping to keep this from escalating. "The police have probably questioned the tenants already. I just want to find out who spoke to the police, what they said and what the police know."

"You don't seriously expect the police to tell you, do you?"

"No, I don't. But that's why I want to talk to the neighbors. If I know what questions they were asked and what their answers were, I might be able to piece together some of this puzzle."

Milt rolled his eyes. "What can I do to make you stop this nonsense?"

"This isn't nonsense." My voice was becoming louder with each word. "This is important to me. Try to understand. I have to do this. I can't pretend that nothing happened."

"Fine," Milt said, giving up the fight, at least for the moment. "You're getting yourself in over your head on this one, Sadie. I don't want you to get hurt."

"I'll be careful. Really." I walked over and gave him a hug. He didn't respond, but he didn't back away either.

As I headed out the door, I thought about Milt and Frannie's comments which frankly, seemed a little over dramatic. All I was going to do was keep in touch with Andy and talk to some of my neighbors.

Okay, so maybe I was spending a lot of time thinking about the sequence of events and who might or might not be suspicious. And maybe I did plan on asking a lot more than a few questions here and there. Still, to hear my family talk, you'd think I was conducting a face-to-face interview with Hannibal Lector in the middle of his kitchen.

Of course I'd be careful. I wasn't that dumb. At least I hoped I wasn't.

CHAPTER SIX

I spent the rest of the afternoon talking to some of the neighbors without turning up anything interesting. No one saw or heard anything unusual after the meeting broke up. Nor did anyone know where Sol, his wife and assistants went at that point either.

I returned to the apartment a little after four. Milt had left me a note saying he had run out to the hardware store and that he'd be back by five.

I checked messages. Andy had not returned my call, so I called again. The woman who answered told me that there had been a double homicide and Andy had been tied up a good part of the day. She did assure me, however, that the homicide team had been actively working Sol's murder and that I shouldn't worry. Ha! She sounded like Milt.

I went next door to see if Mrs. Pinsky had returned from her doctor's appointment. She opened the door as soon as I knocked.

"Oh, I was just on my way to see you." she said. "I heard about the murder. It's all over the news. Come in. My daughter and I stopped at the bakery on the way home. I bought an apple strudel. It's not as good as mine, but it will have to do. I want to talk about the murder. I know who did it."

"What? What do you mean, you know who did it?"

"It was his wife," she answered without a moment's hesitation.

"Sabrina? Why do you say that?"

"Because she never looked happy with Sol." Mrs. Pinsky answered, setting the strudel on the table and filling her teapot with water.

"I don't believe that's considered a strong motive for murder." I said, eyeing the strudel.

"Maybe. Maybe not, she answered, placing a slice of strudel on a plate and handing it to me. "All I'm saying is that Sabrina certainly could be the killer. She's not a nice person."

"Mrs. Pinsky." I tried to reason. "There are a lot of people who aren't nice. That doesn't make them killers. How can you say such a thing?"

"Because that's what I think." Her arms were folded tightly across her chest, her convictions firm and unflappable. "And that's what I told that police detective."

"You told the police that Sabrina killed her husband?" My hand, firmly gripped around a forkful of strudel, stopped in mid-motion.

Mrs. Pinsky nodded.

"What did they say?" I asked, resuming the motion of the fork in my hand as it made its way to my mouth.

"Well, they must have taken me seriously because they told me they'd look into it."

I thought about that for a minute. I also savored the delicious taste of strudel in my mouth. Most of the time I tried to keep my caloric intake in check, but strudel was not easy to resist. Meanwhile, trying to remain focused on Mrs. Pinsky's declaration, I considered the ramifications of her action. I was sure the police would be looking into Sabrina as well as the two men with Sol that evening, so Mrs. Pinsky's comment about the police shouldn't exactly surprise me.

"Is there anything else that makes you think Sabrina's the killer?" I asked between bites.

"No. But, I know I'm right."

I didn't say anything further at this point, choosing to let Mrs. Pinsky continue to prosecute Sabrina without apparently any real evidence to back up her claims. I did however, finish the rest of the strudel on my plate, listening with half an ear to the rest of her ramblings.

I reluctantly resisted her offer of another slice of apple strudel and, after what I hoped was a proper amount of time, told Mrs. Pinsky I had things to do, thanked her and left.

I checked messages again when I got back to the apartment. Andy still had not returned my call and that made me mad. I called again. This time I told the person who answered to let Andy know that his former religious school teacher, just in case he had forgotten, would very much appreciate a call back at his earliest convenience.

Next on my list was a visit to Morris Rubenstein, Sol's father. Besides wanting to make a condolence call, I had several questions I wanted to ask him about the night Sol was murdered. However, going there myself would be awkward. Going with Milt would be better. I'd have to gauge Milt's mood when he returned, to see if he'd be agreeable to going with me later that evening.

Just then, Milt walked in carrying a large shopping bag.

"What did you buy?" I asked. His cheeks were flushed and he looked animated, even happy.

"After our visit with the kids this morning I thought, since Julie likes playing with her dolls so much, I'd build a doll house for her. I bought a kit at the store. It'll be a small one, but I think she'll get a kick out of playing with it next time she visits." He unwrapped the kit and started for his workbench.

I was relieved to see that the walk, the kit and the doll house project, had apparently erased most of Milt's annoyance at me.

Encouraged by his good mood, I suggested going out for dinner, which he accepted. I stopped short of bringing up the idea of making a condolence call to Mr. Rubenstein, thinking it best not to push my luck until later.

We had an early dinner at a seafood restaurant a few blocks from where we lived. Milt talked excitedly about the doll house and the modifications he was going to make to some of the plans. I was thinking that this would be a good time to bring up a condolence call, when Milt surprised me.

Taking a break from his nonstop description of building miniature doors, designing windows that opened and adding a battery operated device for a doorbell, Milt said, "You know, while I was walking back from the store, I was thinking. It probably would be a nice thing for us to stop by Mr. Rubenstein's this evening to offer our condolences. Do you agree?"

Did I agree? If he only knew!

"I think that would be a very lovely and gracious thing to do. I'm so glad you thought of it." I reached across the table and patted his hand.

***

After dinner, with a store bought crumb cake in hand, we knocked on Mr. Rubenstein's door. He lived in a one-bedroom apartment on the first floor. The apartment was quiet, except for the sound coming from the television.

Mr. Rubenstein let us in, gesturing for us to follow him into the living room. The resemblance between father and son was striking, although Morris Rubenstein was a little shorter, a lot thinner and had even less hair than his son.

Mr. Rubenstein walked over to a recliner and sat down, while Milt and I settled on the soft chairs facing him. An evening sitcom had just started, apparently capturing the senior Rubenstein's attention.

"Did you have a lot of people stop by today?" I blurted out, unable to remain quiet.

"Who should stop by?" He asked, eyes staring blankly at the screen.

"Well, I thought maybe some of your family would come."

"What family?" His tone was flat. "My sister and her children live in California. Too far for them to come. No other family. My son, my Solly, he was all I had."

I looked at Milt, nudging him with my eyes. Go ahead, I mentally urged, talk to the man, ask him something.

"I've seen that show," Milt said, nodding towards the television. "It's relatively new and pretty good so far. Do you like it?"

I rolled my eyes. Milt has many attributes, making small talk during a bereavement call, was not one of them.

Mr. Rubenstein turned to look at Milt then returned his stare to the television. After a few moments of silence, he answered in a soft, sad voice. "I don't know what I'm watching. It's on so I don't sit in the dark and cry."

I reached into my purse for a tissue, dabbed at my eyes and cleared by throat. "If you don't mind my asking, Mr. Rubenstein. What are the arrangements for the funeral? Will it be tomorrow?"

"Yes." He said without emotion."

"And are you expecting many people to attend?" I continued.

Mr. Rubenstein turned towards me. "Solly's wife called this morning," he said in an angry voice. "She didn't want a service. No eulogy, no prayers, nothing. 'Nothing but the burial,' she says to me. 'Quick. No one, just us and that's it.'" Mr. Rubenstein blew his nose.

"What did you say then?" I asked feeling both sad for Mr. Rubenstein and angry at Sabrina for being so heartless.

"What did I say? I yelled at her. She yelled at me. We need a *minyan*, I told her. At least ten people should be there to recite the Kaddish prayer. I even explained to her that the Kaddish is the special prayer for the dead. It's not right without a *minyan*. It's disrespectful. It's not kosher. It's not even Jewish."

He paused, sighing heavily before continuing. "'We don't need anything,' she yells back at me. 'He's dead. What difference does it make if there are extra people or not?' I couldn't get her to understand. We both kept yelling at each other. Then she hung up on me."

I listened, wide eyed at what I was hearing. "How could anyone, let alone a daughter-in-law, be so callous, so unfeeling? What is wrong with that woman? You just lost your son, and she shows no respect for either of you."

"Honey!" Milt's voice was raised. "Enough. You're upsetting Mr. Rubenstein."

"No, it's okay. Your wife is right. Sabrina is mean. She's nasty to everyone, especially to me. To Solly she was usually on good behavior. She saw dollar signs in him and didn't push too far. Solly was taken in by her looks, but she has a cold heart and no soul."

I felt subdued for the moment, guilty over my outburst.

"Is there anything we can do, Mr. Rubenstein? Can we help with the funeral?" Milt asked, looking at me.

"Yes," I jumped in, glad to be on another subject. "What can we do?"

"There's nothing to do. Tomorrow I'll have a car service take me to the cemetery and I'll say Kaddish for my son. She can do whatever the hell she wants to do."

"Mr. Rubenstein," I said, hoping Milt would go along with me on what I was about to propose. "Would you mind if Milt and I attended the services with you tomorrow? We'd make arrangements for the car service to take the three of us there."

"You would do that?"

"Of course." Milt answered immediately. I smiled, mouthing a silent 'thank you.'

"Fine," he shrugged. "But it still won't be a *minyan*," he added sadly.

"Well, what if I call Rabbi Solomon at our temple? I bet he'll be able to get a few congregants to make up a minyan. Would that be okay?"

He nodded slowly and closed his eyes. Mr. Rubenstein was getting teary. I didn't want to upset him any more, so I stood to leave, a signal to Milt to do the same. We repeated our condolences, told him we'd knock on his door in the morning, and said goodbye. We walked quietly to the door and let ourselves out.

As we rode the elevator to the fourth floor, I realized I'd forgotten to ask Mr. Rubenstein if Sol had visited him the night of his murder.

"Darn," I was angry at myself for having been distracted by his comments about Sabrina and their phone conversation. "I had questions to ask him and I totally forgot. Besides wanting to know if Sol had stopped by, I wonder if Sabrina was with him. If she wasn't with Sol, then I wonder if she left with the bodyguards or was she waiting with them outside?" I looked over at Milt. He was staring at the elevator ceiling, not looking amused.

"Sorry," I muttered in a soft voice.

"Honestly Sadie, when will you give this murder business a rest?"

Bringing this up in front of Milt had been a mistake. He thought I was getting too personally involved and that annoyed him, which in turn annoyed me. I'd have to be more careful, or at least selective, about sharing my thoughts out loud when I was with him.

"You're right. I won't talk about it any more." At least not to you, I thought, but I didn't share that with him.

"That's not what I mean. It's not just the talking, it's the obsession you're developing with everything, the pending sale, the murder, asking everyone about it, calling your police friend constantly. That's what's getting to me."

Milt unlocked the door to our apartment.

I forced myself to remain silent.

Milt went to his workbench and started laying out the instructions and parts for the doll house. I went to my desk. My mind was racing with questions that I wanted to get down on paper before I forgot most of them. Where had Sabrina gone after the meeting ended? Did Sabrina kill her husband? Would she inherit his money and property? If she did kill him, how did she do it? Did she hire the bodyguards to be paid killers? That was a possibility. But if Sol had been in his father's apartment after the meeting, how would she, or they, have gotten Sol up to one of the higher floors?

"Let me think this through." Without realizing it, I started speaking aloud again. "Sol was a heavy man. Sabrina wouldn't have been able to throw him over the railing by herself. Maybe the bodyguards were in on it as well. Of course they could have killed him downstairs, dragged him up to the fourth, fifth or sixth floor and then dropped him. But what if it was one of the neighbors and not Sabrina?" I continued, my eyes closed, letting my imagination conjure up various murder scenarios. I sighed, opened my eyes and found Milt staring at me.

Without another word, he turned, walked out of the room and, for the first time in a very long time, he slammed the door shut behind him.

"What was that about?" I asked, opening the door and following Milt into the other bedroom where he went straight to his workbench.

"Sorry," he said without turning around. His voice was low and steady, as though he were forcing himself to keep it from getting loud and angry. "I didn't mean for the door to slam quite that hard." He tinkered with a few pieces of wood. "When I see you all wrapped up in this, talking to yourself, so obviously obsessed by what happened, it upsets me."

"I don't know why it would upset you Milt. It's no different than your concentration now with the doll house."

"No." He said, now looking directly at me. "It's very different. That's the problem, you don't see any difference and I can't get you to understand."

This was going nowhere.

"I hear what you're saying and I understand how you feel, but please trust me to know what I'm doing." I felt myself fighting to keep my own anger in check. I stood for a moment, waiting, watching Milt tinker with the same pieces in front of him.

Finally, I turned to leave. "I'll let you get back to what you're doing."

Milt reached for my arm, pulling me gently towards him.

"I love you very much. I don't want us angry at each other," he said softly. "Okay?"

"Okay." I said, feeling some of the tension leave my body. "No one's angry. We're fine and I love you too." I kissed him lightly and walked out.

Once back in the other room, I closed my eyes, counted to ten and breathed deeply. I certainly didn't want to keep walking a tight rope around Milt when it came to my involvement in the police investigation. However, while he might not understand my persistent interest in the police investigation, I was not about to stop and just walk away from it. I cared too much.

This was my building, these were my neighbors, and no one, I whispered to myself, was going to get away with cold blooded murder on my watch.

CHAPTER SEVEN

After a very quiet dinner, Milt went back to tinker with his project. I called Rabbi Solomon and explained Mr. Rubenstein's concern that there might not be enough people at the funeral. The rabbi assured me that he'd make a few calls and bring several members of the congregation with him the next day.

After thanking the rabbi, I called our car service and got that set up. Then I went next door to Mrs. Pinsky to ask if she wanted to go to the funeral with us. It was close to nine when I knocked at her door.

"What is it? Something happen again?" Mrs. Pinsky asked, clutching a dark blue chenille robe tightly around her body.

"No, no" I calmed her down. "Everything is fine. I'm sorry I worried you. It's about Sol's funeral tomorrow morning. I arranged for car service to take us, along with Mr. Rubenstein. I wanted to see if you felt comfortable attending."

"Of course," she answered without hesitation. "If you don't mind *schlepping* one more in the car. It's important to do this for the father, regardless of how I felt about his son."

***

Mrs. Pinsky, wearing a black knit suit that smelled slightly of camphor, and a small black hat with a veil, was waiting at her door when we called for her the next morning.

When we reached the first floor, Mr. Rubenstein was waiting for us near the elevator, hat in hand, ready to go. Not knowing if he had ever formally met Mrs. Pinsky before, I made the introductions. Mrs. Pinsky offered her condolences, and Mr. Rubenstein nodded.

The car service I had called had sent a large car for us, which I was pleased to see was waiting for us when we walked out. Milt sat in front with the driver and I climbed in the back with Mr. Rubenstein and Mrs. Pinsky.

It was overcast when we arrived at the cemetery, although the sun was trying to peek out from behind the clouds. After parking, we walked the short distance to the burial site. A few minutes later several cars arrived and parked behind our car. Mr. Rubenstein's eyes opened wide when he saw the rabbi and his wife walking towards us, followed by a number of people from the congregation.

If Sabrina was less than happy to see the assembled group of mourners when she showed up that morning, she kept her opinion to herself. She briefly acknowledged her father-in-law, gave a hostile look to Milt and me, and ignored everyone else.

While Rabbi Solomon offered a few psalms and prayers, setting the appropriately respectful tone to the proceedings, Sabrina's cell phone rang. Instead of discreetly turning it off, she rummaged in her pulse, found her phone and proceeded to talk to the caller.

"What does she think she's doing?" A very irate Mrs. Pinsky whispered to me. "Her husband's being buried and she doesn't have the decency to wait till after the service to talk to her friends."

"I know. I can't imagine what could be so important that she has to do this here right now."

I found it difficult to concentrate on the rabbi's words because I was trying to hear what Sabrina was saying. Unfortunately for me, she had placed her hand over her mouth as she spoke.

By now the other mourners were casting looks at Sabrina, leaving no doubt of their disapproval. When her cell phone rang again, Mr. Rubenstein gave his daughter-in-law a hard look. Sabrina, returned the glare, rolled her eyes and turned away.

Sabrina's cell phone continued to ring two more times, piquing my interest as to who had called and why. Were these calls connected to Sol's murder or was I just imagining that it was?

When the service ended, Mr. Rubenstein, Milt, and I shook hands with the rabbi, while Mrs. Pinsky made a beeline for Sabrina. Grabbing the cell phone from Sabrina, Mrs. Pinsky yelled. "You have no respect for either your husband or your father-in-law. In fact, you have no respect for anyone but yourself! How could you make phone calls at a time like this?"

Shouting over Mrs. Pinsky's tirade, Sabrina bellowed back as she roughly reached for her cell phone. "You, old lady, should mind your own business. For your information, I wasn't making calls, I was receiving calls. Important calls, I might add."

I started to head in their direction, hoping to either diffuse the situation or, at the very least, ward off potential blows. But it was over as fast as it had begun. Mrs. Pinsky said what she wanted to say and walked away in a huff. Sabrina in turn, finished her response to Mrs. Pinsky and left without so much as a goodbye to anyone, including her father-in-law.

"What was that all about?" Milt asked as we walked to the car.

"I guess Mrs. Pinsky had to let Sabrina know that her behavior was not appreciated," I said as Mrs. Pinsky rapidly approached us.

"Well," I turned to Mrs. Pinsky. "Did you find out who she was talking to?"

"No. Only that the calls were important, or so she said." Mrs. Pinsky stopped to catch her breath.

"I wish I had been able to hear her phone conversation," I said, stopping along side her while Milt continued to the car.

"Me too." Mrs. Pinsky agreed. "I just can't imagine what could have been so important that the calls couldn't wait until after the funeral."

Abruptly, Mrs. Pinsky took my arm and whispered. "I might not have been able to get answers, but I have to tell you, I feel better now that I was able to give her a piece of my mind."

"Good. As long as you feel better." I gave her a hug and we resumed walking.

The drive back was pretty much a carbon copy of the ride to the cemetery. Mr. Rubenstein was quiet, Mrs. Pinsky said she felt exhausted and Milt looked like he could use a nap. I was anxious to get home to see if Andy had returned my phone calls. I knew I wasn't a high priority on his list, but I did expect a courtesy call back.

As we neared the apartment building, Milt yawned and asked if we could stop at the diner on Kings Highway for a quick bite. After the long morning, we all agreed that it was definitely time to eat.

When we finished our lunch, I asked Mr. Rubenstein if he had food in his apartment. My thought was that we'd pick up a few things for him at the diner before heading back.

"I'm fine," he answered. "I have food. I'll manage. You shouldn't worry."

"I have a delicious kugel I'll bring down for you, just so you'll have something if you get hungry later," Mrs. Pinsky said.

"A kugel? That I won't refuse," Mr. Rubenstein answered with a hint of a smile. "If it's not too much trouble."

"What trouble?" She said. "I make a kugel at least once a week. I make enough for eight people and I'm only one. I'll bring you some chicken soup too. I always have that on hand. It has noodles and matzah balls. It's good. You'll like it."

Milt and I looked at each other with amusement as we watched this exchange.

I reached for my purse and was about to stand up when I saw Mrs. Pinsky staring at me in a strange way. Her face had suddenly paled. As I looked her eyes glazed over and her eyelids started fluttering.

"What is it Mrs. Pinsky?" I asked with alarm. "Are you all right?"

She closed her eyes. Leaning to her right, she collapsed on Mr. Rubenstein's shoulder, then slowly slipped to the floor.

A couple sitting at the table next to us jumped up, our server screamed, and several diners shouted for someone to call 911.

Mr. Rubenstein and Milt seemed immobilized by shock.

"She's having a heart attack!" I yelled, running over to her. I knelt down and tried to remember all the first-aid courses I had ever taken. I put my head to her chest and felt, or hoped I felt, a faint pulsing. "She's alive," I called out in a trembling voice. "She's breathing! Oh, thank God, she's breathing."

"Mrs. Pinsky. Can you hear me?" I cradled her in my arms, feeling tears trickle down my face. I couldn't remember if I was supposed to have her sit up or lie flat. All the times I'd heard about these things happening, there was always a doctor around. This time, no one pushed through the crowd of spectators to offer medical assistance.

I lowered my head to her chest again. I was having trouble detecting a heartbeat this time. I didn't know what that meant. Was it because I was too scared to focus or was it so weak I couldn't hear it? I heard the distance wail of the approaching ambulance. "Please, dear God," I prayed. "Don't let her die."

CHAPTER EIGHT

Mrs. Pinsky didn't die, but she had given us quite a scare. The doctor called it 'vasovagal syncope.' He told us it happens when there's a drop in blood pressure which causes a decreased blood flow to the brain, resulting in dizziness or fainting. Fortunately, he had reassured us, this was not considered a serious or life threatening condition.

Mrs. Pinsky was released a few hours later to her daughter, Melinda, who insisted that her mother stay overnight with her.

We had dismissed our driver after he dropped us off at the hospital, so Mr. Rubenstein, Milt and I had taken a cab back to the apartment. After saying good-bye to Mr. Rubenstein, Milt and I went to the lobby to check for mail.

"Poor man," I said. "It must have been very hard for him. First he buries his son, then he finds himself waiting in a hospital emergency room for what could have been another tragic death, God forbid."

"I was thinking the same thing," Milt said. "He was awfully quiet at the hospital and during our ride home."

"I'll stop by later to see if he's okay."

Helen Brunner was just closing her mail box as we approached. She was holding a cluster of magazines and envelopes. We nodded to each other.

"Milt," I whispered. "I want to talk to her, would you mind going up without me and I'll catch up with you a little later?"

"Now?" Milt stared at me. "Can't you do this later?"

"No. Actually, I need to do this right now, while I have the chance. She might not be in later and I want to know why she snubbed me the other day."

"And of course you want to talk to her about Sol's murder, right?"

"Possibly. And if I do, what's wrong with that?"

Milt shook his head. "I don't know why you insist on doing this, but I can tell that I'm not going to change your mind. I'll see you upstairs." He turned and headed toward the elevators.

I walked over to Helen Brunner. She was wearing a gray sweater set with a matching long skirt. Her pale complexion matched her outfit and, for a moment, I wondered if she might be sick.

"Hello," I said. "Terrible, isn't it, Sol Rubenstein's death. What a shock that was. And what a terrible way to die."

She didn't answer. She stood in front of me, fumbling with the mail in her hands.

Oh boy, I thought. The woman obviously didn't want to talk to me, although for the life of me I couldn't figure out what I had done to bring this on.

I turned, intending to walk away with what little dignity I had left.

"Uh, Mrs. Maven," her voice quivered. "Could I talk to you for a moment?"

"Excuse me?"

"This is very awkward for me, but I really don't have anyone else to talk to. It's about the, you know, murder."

She was looking down at the floor. I couldn't tell if her behavior was from shyness, nervousness or both. Could the murder have affected her this badly that she was having a difficult time talking about it? Had she known Sol that well?

"Okay," I answered, not sure whether I should bring up my hurt feelings from her snub, or let her tell me what she had in mind. Not being one to let things fester, I decided to plunge right in to clear the air.

"I have to tell you, Mrs. Brunner, I'm confused. I've tried to talk to you a few times and you've ignored me. Now you're telling me you need to talk. Frankly, I don't understand."

"I ignored you?" She sounded genuinely surprised. "Oh, I'm so sorry." The change in her demeanor was instant. She became contrite, almost childlike in her embarrassment. "Sometimes I get lost in deep thoughts. I must have just spaced out and didn't hear you. Really, Mrs. Maven, I apologize, I would never be that rude. Please, please accept my apology." She started crying, reaching into her purse for a tissue.

"Oh my. Now I feel terrible. I'm sorry I said anything. I shouldn't have. Forget I even mentioned it."

She blew her nose, wiped her eyes and mumbled something I couldn't make out. I gave her a moment to compose herself, then asked. "What is it you wanted to tell me?"

"I'm on my way to the library. I work there, part time, as a librarian." She still seemed agitated. She kept her head down as she continued dabbing moisture from her eyes.

Okay. I waited, hoping she'd get to her point.

"Something's been eating at me and I don't want to put it off any longer," she finally said.

"Put what off?"

She looked nervously around the empty lobby. Taking hold of my arm, she led me over to a corner near the staircase. The crime-scene tape had been removed, but I still felt goose bumps being this close to where Sol's body had been found.

"I was going to knock on your door this morning, but I changed my mind. I didn't know if I should bother you," she whispered tentatively, causing me to move closer to hear what she was saying.

"I wasn't home. Milt and I went to Sol's funeral this morning."

"I see," she said.

"What is it, Mrs. Brunner? How can I help you?"

She stood there, with a faraway look in her eyes.

"Mrs. Brunner?" I waited.

"I know who killed him, or at least I think I do." She suddenly blurted out, looking around again to make sure no one was nearby.

"You know who killed Sol?"

"I'm not a hundred percent certain," she said. "Oh, well, maybe. I guess I'm fairly sure. I mean, if it is who I think it is, I don't know what to do about it."

"Mrs. Brunner, whatever you think you know or suspect, you must tell the police. You have to. Didn't they talk to you today?"

"They came by this morning, but I was out and John was at work. I found their card under the door. I haven't called them. I'm afraid to." Her voice was low and shaky.

"Why are you afraid? What is it, Mrs. Brunner?"

She looked around again, shuffled from one foot to another, closed her eyes, then opened them. When she spoke, her words chilled me to the bone.

"My husband."

"Your husband? You're afraid of your husband?"

"No. Well, yes. What I mean is, I think my husband is responsible for the murder of Sol Rubenstein."

I was stunned. "Why do you think it was your husband?"

"You were at the meeting. Didn't you hear him make those threats?"

"Of course I did. But others were sounding off too. The Dudley boys especially. They were very threatening. I almost thought Chuck was going to start punching Sol. But that was it. Words, fists, that's all. Nothing suggesting murder."

She didn't respond.

I waited a bit before continuing. "What exactly happened that makes you think your husband killed Sol?"

"After John and I returned to our apartment, John said he was going out. He was still angry at Sol. I assumed he went to Dollars, a bar on Avenue U, to cool off, you know."

I didn't know, but I nodded.

"That's what he always does when he needs to blow off steam. Or at least that's what he tells me. This time he didn't."

"He didn't what?"

"He didn't go to the bar."

"How do you know he didn't go?"

"Because I called there and they said he hadn't been in all evening."

"Couldn't he have gone to another bar?"

"That's certainly possible," she said with what sounded to me like irritation in her voice. "However, he always goes to the same one. He's knows the owner. I think they went to school together. Anyway, when John did return, sometime around ten, maybe a little after, he was still agitated. Of course I didn't know about the murder until I heard it on the morning news, so I didn't think much of his mood."

"Did he say anything to you when he came in?"

"He started to, but I pretended to be asleep. I didn't want to say or do anything that would provoke him and make him angrier. Sometimes he takes it out on me. You know he has a temper? I mean I assume everyone who knows John knows that."

Oh my. Here was my neighbor naming her husband as a suspect in Sol's murder. Was she also trying to tell me that her husband's temper could and maybe did get out of hand? Did I know he had a temper? No. Was she implying physical abuse along with his temper? God, I hoped not.

"Was there anything else that makes you suspect your husband?" So far she hadn't mentioned any specific proof. He was angry. He went out. He wasn't where she thought he was. That didn't mean I didn't believe her, it was just that what I had heard, so far, didn't add up to murder.

She looked at me for a few seconds before responding. "John doesn't like to talk about this, but he has mood swings. He can be as sweet as a baby one minute, then, wham, other times he just flies off the handle. I'm not saying I have proof that he killed Sol, I'm just going with my hunch. John was very angry at the meeting, I don't know where he went when he left and, as far as I know, he doesn't have an alibi for the time Sol was killed.

Wow! Frannie had been right. This whole thing was going way beyond helping people find lost keys.

"You've got to tell the police," I pleaded. "Look, I know one of the detectives involved in the investigation. I've been trying to reach him and was actually going to call his office again as soon as I went up. Do you want me to tell him what you just told me?"

"I don't know," she said. "Do you think that would be all right? I mean, you wouldn't mind telling the police for me?"

"No, I wouldn't mind. However, at some point they are going to want to talk to you directly."

"I know, but at least you will have paved the way for me." She looked around again before whispering, "I don't want John to know I told the police about him. He'd kill me, I'm sure of that."

"Kill you?" That sent chills down my spine. "Where is your husband now?"

"He's at work. He'll be home later this evening."

Okay, at least she's safe for now, I thought as I tried to reassure her. "I'll tell the detective what you told me."

"Thank you, Mrs. Maven, I can't tell you what this means to me. I feel as though a huge weight has been lifted from my shoulders."

"Will you be all right?" I touched her shoulder lightly. "I mean, do you want me to come up with you and call from your apartment? Or you can come to mine, while I place the call."

"No. Thank you. I knew you were the right person to confide in. You and your husband look like such nice people, I feel like I can trust you."

"You can." I reached into my purse. I took out a pen and scrap of paper and wrote down my phone number. I handed it to her. "Don't hesitate to call if you need anything, or just want to talk."

"Telling the police for me is a tremendous help," she said as we both walked towards the elevator. She was clearly friendlier and more relaxed now than she had been initially. The irony was that as she seemed to relax more, I started having second thoughts about what I was doing. What if the police didn't arrest John Brunner? What if John was angry at being questioned and found out it had been his wife who suspected him and that by telling me, had led the police to him? Or what if John is innocent and he has to go through the ordeal of being a suspect based on his wife's hunch? *Oy!*

"I was really afraid to make the call." Mrs. Brunner continued talking as my apprehension increased. "But once the police know, then, well, it's out of my hands and I'll deal with whatever happens after that. I can't thank you enough for your help with this. I feel so much better now."

While Mrs. Brunner continued to thank me and tell me how wonderful she now felt, I couldn't get past the 'what if John did in fact have a temper and he came after his wife and me'?

"Mrs. Maven?" Helen's voice brought me back to earth. The elevator had arrived and she was holding back the door for me to enter. I walked in and pressed the buttons to our respective floors, remaining silent the rest of the way up.

When we reached my floor she held on to the elevator door again as I started to walk out. "Mrs. Maven?" She called out to me.

"Yes?"

"I really am sorry, about the, you know, about being rude to you the other day. I don't remember exactly what I was thinking, but I certainly didn't mean to ignore you."

"I understand. Forget about it."

"You're very kind." she said, releasing the door. "Thank you."

I nodded and gave a half-hearted wave. Walking to my apartment I thought how strange this all was. I barely knew the woman. Why had she sought me out to suddenly confide in? Surely there must be other neighbors she knew better.

I had my key out, hesitating before unlocking my door. On one hand, I would have found it very helpful to be able to tell Milt about this latest piece of information. On the other hand, I wasn't that crazy. There was no doubt Milt would be less than pleased to see me this excited over what he perceived as my misguided personal interest in a police investigation.

I heard Milt puttering in the kitchen. A step stool stood in the middle of the room.

"Hi," I said trying to mask the anxiety I felt. "Why is the step stool out?"

"I changed the light bulb," Milt answered. "It was flickering while I was reading the paper." He folded the step stool, placing it back in the pantry.

"Oh. Good," I said, hoping I wouldn't start babbling. I took out the chicken breasts I had defrosted for dinner.

Milt walked over to me and took my hand. "I'm sorry for snapping at you when you wanted to talk to Mrs. Brunner." He said. "It wasn't a big deal and I shouldn't have overreacted the way I did."

"Thank you!" I said, surprised, but pleased. "Apology accepted."

"That's a relief." He smiled. "I didn't think you'd let me off the hook so easily." He hesitated, then asked. "So? What did Helen say about the other day, you know, when she snubbed you?"

"She said she didn't remember doing that, but if she did, she was sorry, that had not been her intention."

"That's it?" Milt asked, looking at me. He knew me well enough to know I was holding out on him.

"Well, she mentioned a few things about her husband having a temper."

"And…." Milt pushed.

"And, she thought maybe he might have had something to do with the murder."

"What?" Milt's eyes opened wide.

"Yeah, hearing her say that caught me by surprise too. Are you hungry? I'm going to broil the chicken. It shouldn't be too long. Want to help me set the table?" That was called a diversionary tactic, one I used often, not always successfully.

"Sadie. Sit down. Tell me what Helen said."

"Why? It's going to upset you. Let's have a peaceful dinner. Then, if you're still interested, I'll tell you later." I took plates and glasses from the cabinet and set them on the table.

"No. Tell me. I promise I won't get upset."

"How can you say that? You got upset when I worried about the pending sale. Then you got upset when I felt emotionally tied to Sol's murder. How can you promise you won't get upset when you don't even know what Helen told me?"

"You're right," Milt agreed. "But the way I see this unfolding is that as long as I know what you know, maybe I can begin to understand what you're thinking. And if I can do that, well then, maybe I won't worry as much. Does that make any sense?"

"No, but I appreciate your attempt." I sat down and patted the chair next to me. "Okay, sit."

I repeated Helen Brunner's story. Milt listened patiently.

"Do you believe her?" He asked when I was through.

"I'm not sure. She could be telling the truth. At least about the temper. You weren't at the meeting, but I certainly saw her husband's angry side. As for his mood swings. It's definitely possible. Why would she make something like that up if it wasn't true?"

"Something's awfully strange about all of this," Milt was shaking his head. "You barely know her, yet when she sees you in the lobby, she suddenly decides to confide in you about something as serious as this."

"I know. It's weird, right? Maybe she felt more comfortable confiding in someone she doesn't know well, instead of someone she does."

"But why you?" Milt continued. "Why now? Why not go directly to the police or wait until she's questioned by them?"

"Good questions, Milt. I don't understand either."

"Maybe there's more to this than she let on. Either she truly believes her husband is the killer or she's angry at him for whatever reason. This could be a 'woman scorned' type of situation where she wants to get back at him."

"Maybe." I said, now completely confused.

The questions reverberated in my head. If John did kill Sol, what was the motive? The pending sale? That didn't make sense. John and Helen both work. If they didn't want to buy into a condo, they could manage to find another apartment. Was Milt right and this was a husband-wife revenge thing? And then there was still the matter of John possibly finding out about Helen's part in this, as well as mine, and the inherent danger that put both of us in.

Of course I couldn't share any of these thoughts with Milt.

I stood up and started pacing.

"Sweetheart," Milt said with some urgency in his voice. "I think it's time you get on the phone and call Andy. Enough of this amateur detecting business. Tell him everything you just told me and let the professionals figure it all out."

Surprisingly enough, I agreed without any argument.

CHAPTER NINE

I called Andy and was told he had still not yet returned to the station. I left my name, again, along with another request that he get back to me as soon as possible.

I busied myself in the kitchen preparing dinner while willing the phone to ring.

When Andy hadn't called by six, we sat down to eat. Milt and I recapped the day, glad that we had been able to offer our support for Mr. Rubenstein, and thankful beyond belief that Mrs. Pinsky's trip to the hospital had turned out okay. There was no mention of Sol's murder.

We finished eating by seven.

"Maybe I should run down to Mr. Rubenstein's apartment to make sure he's all right."

"Wait a few minutes." Milt said. "Your detective friend will most likely call as soon as you leave."

"You're probably right." I went to the freezer and took out two apple turnovers which I placed in the oven to have later with coffee. As I went through the motions, I kept checking my watch every few seconds.

"That's it. I'm calling Andy."

I picked up the phone.

I was put on hold. I drummed my fingers on the counter and mentally prepared the scolding I was going to unload on Andy, once he finally took the call.

After what seemed like an eternity, Andy picked up.

"Mrs. Maven. I'm really sorry about not getting back to you sooner." Andy sounded truly exhausted. "I've been tied up all day with two homicides back to back."

My anger dissipated immediately.

"That's what I was told when I called earlier." I said. "How awful. I don't know how you do what you do Andy, working with killers and dead bodies. Doesn't it get to you?"

"Yeah. Somedays more than others. Look, I just got back." He sounded rushed. "I saw your messages as soon as I sat down. I was about to call you when they told me you were on the line."

"It's okay," I said, now anxious to get right to the point. "Andy, I spoke to my neighbor, Mrs. Brunner. Her husband John, was one of the names I gave you, you know, about the threats at the meeting."

"Yes, I remember. Neither of the Brunners were in when we canvassed the neighbors. You say you spoke to her?"

"Yes. This afternoon. She seemed very upset. She believes her husband killed Sol."

"Really? That's interesting. What makes her think that?" Andy sounded distracted.

I had the feeling that Andy was not taking this information seriously. I wondered if he thought it was hysterics on her part, or mine, for that matter.

"Apparently her husband was upset when they left the meeting," I continued in a rush of words. "She said he left the apartment soon after they returned, telling her that he was going to Dollars, a local bar. Later, she called to see if he was there and was told that John hadn't been in at all."

"Couldn't he have gone to another bar instead?"

"That's what I asked. She told me that Dollars was his favorite hang out because he knew the owner from school. She said that was where John always went when he needed to cool off. Her words, not mine."

"What time did he return to the apartment?"

"According to Mrs. Brunner, it was around ten. She pretended to be asleep when he came back in order to avoid any encounter with him. She told me that John gets moods swings, so he has a tendency to become violent when he's angry. She was afraid that if he was still in, what she called, his mood, it would mean more of his anger directed at her."

"Why didn't she call us?" Andy asked with what I felt was finally a note of urgency in his voice.

"Apparently she's terrified of her husband."

Andy didn't respond. I thought he had become distracted and I was about to say something when he spoke.

"Okay. Thanks for letting me know. I'll check this out. Bye."

"Wait. Andy. Don't hang up." I shouted into the phone.

"Yes?" He answered quickly.

"What about Sabrina and those two henchmen working for Sol?"

"What about them?"

"Are they suspects?"

"Why do you ask? Do you know something we should know about them too?"

"No, but doesn't Sabrina stand to inherit a lot of money and property?"

Not getting any response from Andy, I plowed on. "Until I spoke to Mrs. Brunner, I seriously believed Sabrina could be a suspect. I thought that maybe she hired the guys to kill her husband. And who knows, maybe she's in this with John Brunner and the bodyguards or whatever they're called."

"Mrs. Maven, I didn't know that when you stopped teaching Sunday school you went into the private investigating business," Andy chuckled. "Maybe we should put you on our payroll."

"Andy, are you making fun of me?" I asked in my best Sunday school teacher voice. "Because if you are, I don't appreciate that. John Brunner might or might not be the murderer, but Mrs. Brunner confided her suspicions to me, and I passed them along to you. I also have my own questions regarding Sol's wife and those two men who were with him. I think the least you can do is take all this information seriously and not make fun of my personal involvement." I was miffed.

Maybe he felt guilty for laughing, or maybe it was my Sunday school teacher voice that charmed him, but, bless his heart, he answered my questions. Most of what he told me had probably made its way to the media by that point, but nevertheless, I was happy to hear it directly from him.

After clearing his throat, and apologizing, Andy continued in a more formal tone. "Sabrina Bellina Rubenstein was the first person we spoke to that evening. She went home without her husband. The bodyguards, or assistants, as they like to be called, accompanied her to the Manhattan residence in a cab they called for from their cell phone. The doorman saw her, the elevator guy saw her, and the neighbor across the hall was just coming back from walking his dog, so he can verify her alibi as well."

"But what about later, you know, what did the two guys do after dropping Sabrina off?" I kept pushing for more information, no matter what Andy thought of my persistent inquiries into his police investigation.

"What do you mean?"

"Well, do they have alibis?" I asked. "What if Sabrina paid them to kill Sol. Couldn't one or both of them have returned to the apartment building after dropping her off?"

"Anything is possible, but their story checks out." He took a deep breath, exhaling deeply. "They both have witnesses who saw them enter their respective apartments, one in Manhattan, the other in Brooklyn."

"Oh." I said.

"Oh? You sound disappointed."

"No. Well, maybe yes. I was so sure it was Sabrina. I hate to think it's one of our neighbors though. Then again, if John Brunner did kill Sol, what if he didn't do it alone? What if there's someone else involved and that person goes after John's wife because he or she thinks Helen Brunner knows too much? Her life could be in danger." I felt my heart pounding and my voice getting louder.

"You shouldn't be worrying yourself about this. This is our job. We're pretty good at it too, at least most of the time. Let us take over from here. Okay?" His voice was strained.

"Okay." I answered somewhat petulantly. I wasn't happy that Andy was now dismissing my concerns so casually.

"You still sound disappointed," Andy added. "Don't be. You've helped us a lot with this information."

I understood that he was trying to make me feel better. However, I was not about to take myself out of the loop. These were my neighbors, after all. I worried about how this affected them. I felt devastated over Sol's death, concern for his grieving father and now, Helen Brunner's safety. There was no way I could or would distance myself from the people involved in this tragedy.

I hung up the phone and walked over to the kitchen table where Milt had been listening to my conversation. I rubbed my hand over my forehead. "I'm getting a headache."

"Andy didn't buy your Sabrina theory, did he?" Milt asked. "Now you're worried about Mrs. Brunner, right? Sadie. I know I've said this before, but I'm going to say it again. You can't take on the problems of the world single-handedly. Let the police do their job."

"That's what Andy said, but I can't let it go. And yes, I'm worried about Helen."

Milt got up and took my hand, pulling me up close to him. He hugged me, stroking my back. "You're a good person, Sadie, you know that? Everything will be all right. You'll see. Now come on, where's that dessert you promised me?

"Oh my God!" I shrieked. "The dessert. I completely forgot about that." I grabbed a pot holder, opened the oven door and was blasted by hot steam. After removing the pan, which I placed on the counter, I looked at Milt sheepishly. "Burnt dessert anyone? House special. Two badly blackened apple turnovers."

We never did make it to Mr. Rubenstein's apart-ment that evening. With everything that had happened during the day, I should have seen it as an omen. Of course I naively assumed a funeral, Mrs. Pinsky being rushed to the hospital, Mrs. Brunner's accusation con-cerning her husband, and then burnt dessert was just another one of those days.

CHAPTER TEN

The next day was Saturday, a warm, sunny day that held the promise of spring's arrival. My plan was to get up at six, while Milt was still asleep. I would tiptoe to my desk in the other room and update my 'Sol Rubenstein' file, on paper at least, so as not to disturb Milt with computer noise.

I got as far as my desk. My bare foot hit the side of the desk. I let out an involuntary yelp, and Milt woke up.

"Honey? You okay?" He called out from the bedroom, groggy but obviously alarmed.

"Yes, I'm fine." I growled. "I just stubbed my toe. Go back to sleep."

"What are you doing up this early anyway?"

"Just going over a few things."

He stayed in bed for another minute or two before he got up and came into the room where I was sitting, massaging my toe. He yawned and stretched as he walked over to the window.

"It looks like it's going to be a beautiful day. How about we take a walk to Break Fasts. If we get there early enough, we'll beat the usual mid-morning crowd."

Break Fasts was a favorite of ours, specializing in breakfasts only. It was located three blocks from our apartment building and made for a nice, leisurely walk. Today however, I really wanted to get a handle on everything that had occurred since Sol's murder. I wanted to talk to Helen Brunner and find out what happened after I relayed her suspicions to Andy. Did the police come to their apartment? What was John's reaction? And how were they doing now? I still wanted to check in on Mr. Rubenstein to see how he was. On the other hand, I didn't want to not go with Milt and have him angry at me again for my over-the-top passionate insistence on staying involved.

Milt was waiting for my response.

"Sure, sweetheart." I said, mentally pushing my agenda to the back burner. "That would be great."

I reluctantly returned to the bedroom, got dressed and tried to mute all the 'Sol Rubenstein' thoughts and questions that were running through my mind. Besides not wanting to incur any more of Milt's wrath, I tried to convince myself that it actually might be good to think of other things for a change!

Break Fasts was a tiny storefront almost hidden between a Thai restaurant and a tailor shop. We took a leisurely walk and arrived at the restaurant around eight, our morning newspapers in hand. Milt had been right about getting there early. We were told there'd be less than a five minute wait.

"Well, look who's here." A familiar voice called out.

We turned to see our neighbors, Tony and Carol Lucas, walking out of the restaurant holding hands and smiling.

In their early thirties, the Lucas's had been married for six months, making them still newlyweds in our opinion. Tony, literally tall, dark and prince-charming handsome, worked as an emergency-room doctor in Brooklyn. Carol, model thin with red hair and freckles, was a kindergarten teacher at the neighborhood elementary school.

"Isn't it a great day to be out?" Carol said with her usual cheerful tone.

"Yes," Milt said. "That's why we're out and about early. Don't want to miss a minute of the day."

"So what do you guys think of the latest news on our building's infamous murderer?" Tony asked.

"What news?" I held my breath.

"It's in today's paper. The police arrested John Brunner last night," Tony told us. "I actually saw it happening. It was around ten. I worked late and when I came home I saw John, in handcuffs, being led out of the building by the police. Honestly, it was like watching a taping of one of those crime shows."

"Was his wife with him?" I asked.

"She was walking a few feet behind him, crying. John was pretty much surrounded by the cops, so she couldn't get too close to him."

"Did he say anything?" Milt asked.

"He was yelling, saying he didn't do anything, that they had the wrong guy. The police were telling him to quiet down."

"Was anyone else there, from the building, I mean?"

"There were a few neighbors in the lobby, watching," Tony continued. "He was making a lot of noise. It obviously attracted a good deal of interest."

"Does the paper give any more information on the arrest?" I asked.

"Not really," Carol answered. "You'll see. It's a small article with just the basic information." She looked at her husband. "Honey, tell them about Pete and Chuck."

"The Dudleys?" I asked. "What do they have to do with John's arrest?"

"I'm not sure it had anything to do with the arrest, but there's another article in the paper that says the police don't know where the Dudley brothers are and they're interested in talking to them." Tony explained. "It's not exactly spelled out in the article, but I had heard that apparently someone from the building had seen the two men arguing after the meeting and over-heard one of the brothers say something like, 'They might find out, maybe we should wait.' Whoever heard that probably told the police who, of course, now want to see what that was all about."

"That's interesting." I said. "I saw them leave the meeting in a bit of a huff, but now that I think about it, I haven't seen them since."

"Well, what do you make of John being arrested? Could he really have killed Sol?" Tony asked.

"Who knows?" Milt answered. "I guess if the police arrested him, they must have something on him. What about you Tony, what are your thoughts?"

"Don't know. But I'll tell you this though, whoever did it, I hope they put him or her away for a long time. From what I hear, the way Sol died was pretty brutal."

"Carol, you were at the tenant meeting, weren't you?" I asked. "What do you think?"

"I was at the meeting, but I didn't stay very long once the yelling started. It was like a bunch of my kindergarten kids on a rainy day with no recess." Carol said. "To be honest, I don't know what to think."

Just then our name was called, unfortunately ending our exchange and my hope of getting Carol's insights into John's arrest. I made a mental note to follow up with a call to her as soon as I could.

We said our goodbyes and Milt and I walked into the restaurant.

"Well, the police sure acted fast on that one," Milt whispered as we were shown to our table. When I didn't respond, he looked at me. "What? What's the matter?"

I waited until the server had left before answering. "Nothing. It just seems like it all happened so fast. Maybe, too fast."

"What do you mean? You gave that detective friend of yours a good lead. He obviously did some checking, followed up with some questioning and decided there was enough to arrest the guy. So that should put an end to this whole murder thing. Over and done." Milt picked up his menu.

"Maybe." I said.

"Maybe? You're kidding, right? Milt said with disbelief. "No, you're serious. My God, Sadie. Give it up already. If the police feel they have the right guy, why are you still belaboring it?"

"You're right, forget I said anything." I had voiced my thoughts again, without thinking. No use getting into this with Milt now. I picked up my menu.

After we had ordered, Milt opened the newspaper, going directly for the sports and business sections. He handed me the national and local news.

I saw the headline immediately. '*John Brunner Arrested For the Murder of Apartment Owner, Sol Rubenstein.*'

"Milt, listen to this." I read the article to him.

> *John Brunner, a sales representative for Walkers, Inc., a national shoe-manufacturing company, was arrested last night at his apartment in Brooklyn, for the alleged murder of Sol Rubenstein, owner of Rubenstein Properties, Inc., a real estate corporation that buys and sells apartment buildings in Brooklyn and Queens.*
>
> *Police report that they were following up on a tip from an undisclosed source indicating that Brunner had made threatening remarks to Rubenstein during a tenants meeting on Wednesday evening. Rubenstein was found dead later that evening from multiple wounds to his head.*
>
> *Neighbors said they had expected Rubenstein, who was in the process of selling the apartment building on Avenue S and East 14th Street, to attend the meeting to explain the sale and offer some assistance. "But he didn't offer us anything," Jake Fischer, one of the building's tenants, stated. "He was arrogant, smug, and not at all interested in the well-being of his loyal tenants."*

"Uh, oh!" I put the paper down.

"What is it now?" Milt asked. I heard the annoyance in his voice and should have stopped right there. As usual, I didn't listen to my instincts and plowed on.

"It says here that an undisclosed source provided the tip."

"So? What's the problem?"

"So, maybe the undisclosed source could be traced back to me, or even Helen. That would be terrible."

"Sadie, your intense preoccupation in this whole business is what's terrible. Whether or not John knows, or anyone else knows, is not the problem." Milt picked up the newspaper and continued reading.

Ignoring his comment, I resumed reading.

> *Detective Andy Cohen, Homicide Division, would not comment on the case, saying only that they had found enough evidence to arrest John Brunner on suspicion of murder.*

I sat for a moment, trying to digest what I had just read. "Oh. Here's the article Tony was talking about." I said, as my eye caught another headline adjacent to the article I had just read.

> *"Missing Brothers Sought By Police*
> *The police are looking into the disappearance of Chuck and Pete Dudley, brothers who live at the same apartment building on Avenue S and East 14th Street, where the owner, Sol Rubenstein, was found murdered last Wednesday. According to the police the men have not been seen since then. While the police insist the two men are not suspects in the murder at this point, the police are interested in talking to them.*

"Milt, do you think something bad happened to them?"

"What? Now you're going to get all worked up over Chuck and Pete?" Milt put his newspaper down and gave me a hard look. "I don't understand you. We keep going around and around on this. And for what? What are you accomplishing? Helen thinks her husband killed Sol. She tells you, you tell Andy and John gets arrested. Okay. Good. So now that's all wrapped up. It's over. Let's move on. But no, you have to keep pressing, wondering, worrying. Why, Sadie" Why is it so important to you?"

I waited until our server placed our food in front of us.

"It's important because I care about these people." I said, feeling like a child explaining a misbehavior.

"I know you care. But sometimes you have to step back and let things play out." Milt picked up the paper and continued to read while he ate.

"Are you very angry at me?" I asked, feeling tears welling up in my eyes.

"I am angry Sadie, not at you, but at what you're doing to yourself, to us."

I picked at my food, unable to eat. I thought about the articles, John's arrest and Milt's reaction. I went from feeling sad that I had upset Milt, to feeling angry at him for not being more supportive. And to think I had given up my plans for the day to please him!

We didn't see Carol and Tony when it was time to leave, which was just as well. The icy chill between Milt and me would have been easily detected by them and difficult to explain.

Milt's questions had resonated deeply with me. Why had I made myself positively insane with this whole murder business? The police had arrested the killer. If two men I barely knew were missing, why did I feel compelled to worry about them? To add to my emerging misgivings, I had begun to feel that, maybe, things had moved too quickly and were now spinning out of control.

The questions twisted and turned in my head. Unfortunately I didn't have any answers. If I had had even a few of the answers at that point, my life would have been a whole lot easier going forward.

CHAPTER ELEVEN

Milt and I walked home in relative silence. We made a few inane comments about the weather, the traffic, and the 'for sale' sign on one of the homes we passed along the way that had not been there earlier. Personally, I was losing my patience and energy with the continuing verbal discord bouncing back and forth between us.

When we exited the elevator on our floor, Mrs. Pinsky was waiting at our door.

"Mrs. Pinsky?" I asked. "What are you doing here? I thought you were with your daughter? Are you okay?"

"I'm fine, I'm fine." She answered, looking a bit frazzled. "My daughter brought me back a little while ago and just left. She was driving me crazy, fussing over me constantly. Besides, I was anxious to come home. I like sleeping in my own bed."

Milt had the door open by now.

"Do you want to come in?" I asked.

"No thanks. I heard about that Brunner fella being arrested and I just want to find out what's going on."

"This is where I say goodbye." Milt said, nodding to both of us before walking into the apartment.

"What did he mean by that? Is he upset at something?" Mrs. Pinsky asked.

"No, he's fine. He just gets annoyed when I'm, what he calls, obsessing with this police investigation."

"Oh. Well, I won't keep you, but I have to tell you that I wasn't all that surprised when I heard the news. I thought it might have been John Brunner all along."

"How can you say that? You told me you were certain it was the wife? Remember?"

"I said that? No, I don't remember. Maybe I was kidding."

"Kidding?" I rolled my eyes.

"Okay. So maybe I did think it was Sabrina. But that Brunner guy was my next choice. There was just something about him. I could never put my finger on it. He had a suspicious look about him that I didn't like."

"A suspicious look?"

Before she could answer, Milt opened the door and came out carrying a fairly large box.

"I need to make copies of my tax files for my appointment with the accountant on Monday." He said. "I should be back in an hour."

"I need to be going, too." Mrs. Pinsky said to both of us. "I'm still feeling a little tired from everything that happened." She waved and headed to her apartment. Her suspicions already forgotten.

Milt gave me a quick kiss on the cheek and went to the elevator as I headed inside.

I decided this would be a good time to call Andy. The less Milt saw or heard of my personal involvement, the less stress there would be for both of us.

I was put through to Andy right away.

"Good morning," he said, sounding relatively upbeat for a homicide detective in the heart of Brooklyn. "I was going to call you today to tell you we appreciated your tip, Mrs. Maven. That was a good call."

"Well, good, I guess."

"You guess?" Andy asked, sounding surprised by my response.

"No, I'm glad, really. Actually I'm curious to know what happened after I spoke to you. How did it all take place? I mean, you said you intended to go to their apartment to talk to them both, but what led you to actually arrest him right then?"

"You're putting me on the spot here. I probably broke every rule in the police manual when I told you as much as I did the last time we talked. I can't do that again. You know I can't give out details of an ongoing investigation."

"I know that," I said in what I hoped was a concili-atory voice. "I'm not asking for confidential informa-tion, only what you feel comfortable sharing. Please, Andy." I knew I was pushing the envelope, hoping once again, that our past relationship as teacher and student, even the fact that I knew his mother, would sway him enough so that he'd give me some information.

There was a long pause.

"Here's what I can tell you. The Brunners were both jumpy when Brian and I went to their apartment. Brian talked to the wife in the kitchen, I stayed in the living room with John. Bottom line is that John didn't have an alibi for that time frame and his threatening remarks to Sol Rubenstein, which you pointed out, were heard by everyone at that meeting. That was enough for us to feel comfortable taking him down to the station for more questioning."

"But the newspapers said he was arrested. That's more definite than just being held for questioning. Right?"

"We're still investigating." Andy's voice was tight.

"What about his motive?" I persisted.

"I can't answer that."

"But if he is guilty, how did he kill Sol and why? Was there a weapon involved? John couldn't just lift him up and throw him over the railing of the stairs. Sol was short, but he would have fought him."

"I'm sorry. That's all I can and will answer." Andy's voice was now quite testy. "Where's this all going anyway, Mrs. Maven? I thought you agreed you wouldn't remain permanently involved anymore."

"I'm just curious, Andy." I said, wondering what had given him the idea that I wouldn't remain permanently involved with the investigation. "That's all it is. Certainly there's nothing wrong with that now, is there?"

"If being curious is all it is, then sure, I suppose it's okay."

"But…" I whispered.

"But….?" Andy challenged.

"But, I do have just one more little question."

"Oh boy! With you there isn't any such thing as a little question."

"Why are the police interested in the Dudley brothers?" I asked, ignoring Andy's comment. "Was it because they made threatening remarks? Were they working with John Brunner? Is there some concern for their safety?"

"Whoa! Was that your idea of one little question?

"I'm sorry. I appreciate the fact that you've shared as much information with me as you have. It's just that I heard that someone from the building saw Chuck and Pete arguing outside the lobby soon after the tenant meeting that Wednesday."

"So?"

"So, is that why you're interested in them? Is it because they were overheard arguing or because no one has seen them since?"

Andy didn't answer.

"Please, Andy. Just answer this question and I won't bug you any more." Of course I meant for today, but that was a little detail I didn't think was worth mentioning at this point.

Still no response. I held my breath.

"Okay, but this is it. We've been trying to get in touch with them since Wednesday night. Right now it's a loose end. We just want to talk to them. That's all. Now, I've answered your question and I need to get back to work."

I knew I had pushed as far as I could. I thanked Andy and hung up.

I grabbed my keys with the intention of seeing if Helen Brunner was in. I hoped she was okay, considering the trauma of last night. Before I reached the door, the phone rang. Like Pavlov's dog, I'm conditioned to answer ringing phones.

"Hello." I said, hoping it was a wrong number so I wouldn't get stuck on the phone the rest of the morning.

"Hi, is this Sonja? It's Bill. Bill Lancaster, I worked with Milt for years before we both decided to pull the plug and retire."

"Bill, oh, of course." It took me a moment for his name to register. Bill was one of Milt's retirement buddies.

"How've you been?" I asked, looking at my watch.

"Fine, fine. And you, your family?" Bill asked in return.

"Great, Bill. Thanks. Uh, I'm sorry, I hate to do this, but I'm on my way out and Milt won't be home until this afternoon. Can I have him call you later?"

"Oh, gee, I'm sorry. Sure." Bill said. "Tell the old man it's time for another lunch." Bill laughed.

Three or four times a year, a group of Milt's friends from his pre-retirement days got together for lunch to catch up on each other's golf games, fishing expeditions, grandkids and travel plans. Milt always looked forward to those gatherings.

"I will." I was about to add 'bye' and hang up, when Bill spoke again.

"Uh, Sonja? Just one more thing. I wanted to ask Milt about the guy in your building who was arrested for the murder of that real estate tycoon. I think his name was Rubenstein or something."

"Right," I answered. "Sol Rubenstein. Did you know him?"

"No." Bill hesitated. "But I have a neighbor who says he was in the Marines with that Brunner guy, the one they say killed Rubenstein."

"Really?"

"We live right next door to each other. Turns out we were both getting our papers from the driveway this morning, at the same time. My neighbor opens the papers, right there on the driveway, and sees the headlines and starts talking to me about how he knows the guy. I said, no kidding, and he says, 'Yeah, knew him in the Marines.' He says Brunner was your typical mean, lean, fighting Marine, but an overall nice guy. Played by the rules, you know. Had a temper, but didn't easily get riled up a lot."

"What else did he say?" I was hanging on every word.

"Well, that was about it. Except that he was surprised to hear that John had been arrested for murder. He kept saying how nice the guy was. Oh, he says he knew he was capable of killing. Hell, he says he was trained to do that, but not civilians and not in cold blood like that, you know, like throwing someone over the stairs. I mean, that's what the news anchors are saying now, that the dead guy was thrown from one of the top floors. He says that just doesn't sound like something that the John he knew, would ever do."

Wow! Suddenly I wasn't quite as anxious to get off the phone.

"Did your neighbor think it might have had anything to do with John's days as a Marine. You know, maybe it was one of those delayed trauma things where bad memories lay dormant for years, then snap, they come back and make you do strange things."

"Nah, he didn't say anything like that. But, from what I heard, the police say they have pretty good evidence on this guy, so maybe. You never know. I guess anything's possible. Hey, I'm sorry I'm taking up so much of your time. Have Milt give me a call when he has a chance. Good talking to you. Take care." He hung up.

Bill's call had me thinking of John Brunner in a different light. Until now I had only Helen's comments to go on. I had taken her at her word without giving it a second's thought.

Were Helen's accusations incorrectly based on suspicions? Did we both jump to the wrong conclusions, setting John up in the eyes of the police? If so, how come the police arrested him? And what's with the police and their interest in the Dudley boys? Could there be a connection here?

I took a deep breath, letting it out slowly.

Nothing was making sense to me anymore and I didn't have a clue as to what I would do next. I should have thrown away my 'Sol Rubenstein' file, left the questions for the police to figure out, and returned to my peaceful, somewhat uneventful life.

That would have been easy and certainly the smart thing to do.

But, of course, easy and smart were not the path I chose to take.

CHAPTER TWELVE

I needed more answers. I locked my apartment door and took the stairs up the two flights to Helen Brunner's floor. I knocked first, then impatiently went for the doorbell. I heard footsteps and waited. Helen was smiling broadly when she opened the door. Seeing me, she looked startled, then abruptly her demeanor changed to what I could only describe as her librarian look, quiet, polite, but subdued. She was wearing a white cashmere turtleneck, a long black shirt and black boots. She had obviously done something with her hair and makeup because she looked, well, terrific. Certainly not the grieving look of a woman who had just fingered her husband, then watched as he was hauled off to jail.

"Oh! I was expecting a friend of mine." Helen stammered. "I mean, I'm having lunch with an old classmate from college. I thought you were, um, her. I'm sorry." She opened the door wider. "Would you like to come in?"

I nodded and followed her inside.

The apartment was one-bedroom, simply furnished, neat and uncluttered, with a large sofa, an easy chair, ottoman and coffee table in the living room. The kitchen and bedroom were off to the right.

She pointed to the sofa. I sat down.

"Can I get you something? With everything that has happened, I haven't really shopped lately, but I do have some cold drinks if you want. I might even have some juice, but I afraid that's about it."

"No, thank you though." I answered, feeling awkward at having dropped in on her. I hadn't thought that would be a problem, but now that I was here, I was second guessing myself again. "I just stopped by to see how you're doing."

"Oh. Well, that's nice of you." She ran her fingers through her hair. It was no longer straight, but curly.

"I see you curled your hair. It's very becoming."

"I, um, I did it myself this morning." She answered, but looked away. "I'm very unsettled and nervous about John, you know, the cops coming and arresting him. I needed something to do. It's been rather unpleasant."

"Right," I said, thinking her choice of the word, unpleasant, seemed a bit of an understatement, considering all that had happened in less than 24 hours. "I'm sure it must have been very traumatic. Do you feel like talking about it?"

"Yes, I suppose so." Her tone seemed indifferent. "It's been like a bad dream. I keep expecting to wake up and find John sitting right here with us."

"I can't even begin to imagine how difficult this must be for you." I offered. "I'm so sorry."

"It's just that everything happened so fast." She was playing with her hair as she spoke. "Of course, after you and I had our little discussion, I was expecting the police. But when they came, it was like, oh my, this is for real. I started wondering if I had done the right thing."

"What happened after the police showed up?"

"Two detectives knocked on our door last night." She inhaled deeply, then exhaled before continuing. "They said they were canvassing the neighbors to see if anyone saw or heard anything that might help them with their investigation. John was very tense and uptight, but he had no choice, so he let them in."

"What happened then?"

"At first the detectives talked to both of us at the same time. John admitted that he wasn't sorry Sol had been killed, because selling the apartment just like that was a big problem for the neighbors. He called Sol a rich bastard, said he deserved to die because he was making money off the poor working people."

"He said all that?"

"Yes."

"What was their reaction?"

"The detectives asked him out right if he had had anything to do with the murder." Helen continued. "Of course he denied it. They asked if he had made any threatening remarks to Mr. Rubenstein. John told them he had been angry, but that he didn't remember exactly what he had said."

"Did they believe him?"

"I don't think so. One of the detectives asked to speak to me in the kitchen, while the other one said he had a few more questions and asked John to stay behind in here."

"Then what?" I prompted.

"Next thing I knew, John was yelling that he had nothing to do with any murder and why were they arresting him. The detective and I rushed out of the kitchen. John was already handcuffed. I started crying. I felt so terrible."

She was sniffling, dabbing her eyes and nose with a tissue she pulled from her pocket. I waited for her to continue.

"I'm so sorry Mrs. Brunner. This must have been terribly hard for you."

She nodded. Then she stood up and started pacing. "John continued ranting and raving as we walked out of the apartment. By now some of the neighbors had their doors open and were watching us get into the elevator. When we got to the ground floor, there was several police officers in the lobby, along with people from the building. It was humiliating."

She stopped pacing, blew her nose, and looked away. Then she started pacing again. "You know, the worst part of this is that I feel so guilty."

"Guilty? You shouldn't feel guilty about any of this. You did the right thing by letting the police know. If your husband did do this, the police would have found out sooner or later."

"I suppose you're right. It's just that I feel sorry for him. John's job was in jeopardy because of the economy and I know he was taking it hard. But still, to kill someone, I mean, that's awful. Yet, I can't help thinking that the police would not have arrested John if they didn't have some proof. Maybe it wasn't just what I suspected, maybe they had their suspicions about him too. Don't you agree?"

"I'm sure that's right,"

Helen looked at her watch. I took the hint, thankful for the excuse to leave.

"Well, I said I as I stood up. I'd better get going."

"Thank you for stopping by. I appreciate your concern."

"You're welcome." I answered carefully. "I hope you enjoy your visit with your friend."

"Yes. My friend. Thank you."

I nodded, intent on keeping my mouth shut so I wouldn't blurt out anything I'd later regret. As I turned towards the door, I passed a small table just outside the kitchen. It held a telephone, notepad, a few papers and a clock. Resting on the floor, next to the table, was a baseball bat. Helen must have seen me looking at it because she hurried over to it and picked it up.

"I bought this when I ran out to get the stuff for my hair this morning. I feel embarrassed that you saw it, but I'm afraid to be here alone. I bought it for protection. You know, a woman alone," she laughed nervously.

"Oh." I said, unable to think of anything more intelligent to say. "Right. That's probably good thinking on your part. I guess I'd do the same thing if Milt was away."

She opened the door. We exchanged awkward goodbyes and I left.

I felt unsettled by my visit. Helen was surprised to see me. I could understand that, she was expecting someone else. She had changed her appearance dramatically. But so what? I needed to back off and give the woman a break. Her husband had just been arrested on murder charges. The whole arrest thing had to have been upsetting to her. But what did I know? I couldn't begin to understand what was going through her head.

As it was, I wasn't even sure I understood what was going on in mine!

CHAPTER THIRTEEN

I returned to the apartment. Milt had called while I was gone, leaving a message that he would pick up some deli sandwiches for us before heading home. His message was brief, his tone, neutral. Maybe the chill between us was warming a bit. Hard to tell at this point.

I felt restless. I decided I'd get some exercise at the park across the street. The city had added a par course, and while I didn't follow the course exactly, it was a good opportunity to stretch and bend at my own pace.

I quickly changed into workout clothes and sneakers. I wrote a short note to Milt, telling him where I'd be. I taped the note to the television where I was certain he'd find it.

The weather had turned cold, but it felt good to be outside. Apparently a lot of people felt the same way. The park was full. Children, with their usual level of high energy, were riding tricycles, climbing on the jungle gym, or throwing balls to each other. Parents were sitting nearby, watching or talking among themselves, while keeping a close eye on their kids.

As I walked towards the par course, I saw Carol Lucas. She was doing a few warm up stretches when I approached.

"Hi there." Carol called out. "I see we have the same idea."

"It seems so." I laughed. "Do you use the par course often?"

"Not often enough, although I try to squeeze exercise in whenever I can. If Tony's not on call on the weekends we'll sometimes run together on the track. That's where he is now. I can't keep up with him and I don't like to slow him down, so most of the time I use the course."

"Carol, do you mind if I ask you about John Brunner's arrest? I wanted to this morning at Break Fasts, but then our table was ready and we had to go in."

"Sure, Mrs. Maven. Ask away." She stopped stretching to give me her full attention.

"I'm curious to know what you think about John's arrest. Could he have killed Sol Rubenstein? I mean, did you know John at all? Did he seem aggressive or mean?"

"To be honest, Mrs. Maven, I'm not sure how to answer that." She hesitated before continuing. "The thing is, I sort of know John. He used to come to my school as a volunteer to read to the students. You know that program we have, where the community is invited to help out in the schools with various volunteer programs?"

"Yes. I've read about it. So John is a volunteer at your school?" Once again, I was hearing another side of the man, making me even more aware of how one sided my original perception of him might have been.

"Yes. Well, he was. He actually hasn't been in for a few weeks. He called to let me know he was having a tough time getting the time off from work. He was afraid he'd lose his job if he continued to volunteer."

"Oh, I see. What was John like as a volunteer?"

"The kids loved him. He'd read to them, then he'd tell them about his days in the Marines. They ate it up, called him a hero and all that. Somehow that image doesn't jive with him as a suspected cold blooded killer."

I nodded. A second positive endorsement didn't necessarily mean he wasn't the killer. After all, the police had arrested him. Still, hearing Carol's assessment did add to my growing unease that something wasn't right.

"Apparently he does have a temper." I said. "Maybe he just snapped."

"I've heard about his temper, but I never saw it first hand." Carol said. "Did you?"

"No." I answered. "I really didn't know either of the Brunners very well before all this happened. What's your take on Helen Brunner?"

"I've met her a few times when she was with John. I don't like to say negative things about anyone, but I'm sorry, I found her very strange. I don't know why, but I never felt comfortable around her."

"I know what you mean." I stood quietly, digesting what Carol had said.

After a moment or two, Carol began her warm up stretches.

"Well, I guess I'd better get back to my workout or I'll be here all day gabbing." Carol said as she smiled, waved and walked on to the next exercise station.

I did a few neck rolls, arm circles and legs bends, before moving on to the various stations. I half-heartedly followed the posted instructions indicating the correct form, stance and position for each exercise. Truthfully though, my concentration was less on each stretch, bend and pull, than it was on what Carol and I had just discussed.

I went through a few of the stations before deciding I had had enough. I waved at Carol, who had now joined her husband near the track. Tony was putting on his hooded sweatshirt and Carol was drinking from her water bottle. They waved back.

I headed for the street, about to cross when I saw Milt approaching about a block away. Not knowing that I was at the park, he wasn't looking in my direction, but I waved anyway.

I might have been distracted at that moment by any number of things, waving to Milt, thinking of Carol's comments followed so closely on the heels of Bill's call or my visit to Helen. Seeing Milt carrying his box of tax materials in one hand and the deli bag in the other, could have reminded me of how happy I was to see him and how much, in spite of my frustrations with him at times, he still made my heart soar with love for him. Truth is, I don't remember what had specifically distracted me. What I do recall is suddenly hearing the surging roar of a car engine. Looking around I saw a car rapidly heading straight towards me.

It took several seconds for my brain to process it all. I stood, shocked and frozen in that moment. Then I heard loud shouting coming from behind me and felt someone pull me back to the curb. I landed hard on my elbow, which took the brunt of the fall. I watched, dumb stricken, as a large black sedan sped past me without stopping or slowing down.

A large crowd had formed, creating a circle around me. Carol and Tony were at my side, as well as Milt, who was panting from having run to me after first hearing, then seeing, what had just occurred.

"Are you all right?" I could hear the panic in Milt's voice.

"You need to get this x-rayed," Tony said as he gently checked my elbow.

"Oh my God! Mrs. Maven." Carol said. "That car came right at you. Whoever was driving could have killed you."

"He didn't even stop." I heard someone in the crowd call out.

"What kind of idiot drives like that in front of a park filled with children?" Another spectator added.

I felt dazed and bewildered. Nothing made any sense as I tried to get my bearings. In the background of my mind, I heard the sounds of approaching sirens.

Paramedics swarmed over me. Someone said I needed to go to the hospital. I vaguely remember saying no, in spite of Milt's insistence and Tony's concern.

"Except for my elbow hitting the pavement, nothing feels broken." I recall saying. "I'm not bleeding." I reached out my good arm. "Help me stand up."

Milt and Tony did and I took a quick inventory of all my body parts.

"I'm fine." I said, slowly coming out of my haze. "I promise I'll have my elbow checked out, but I don't want to go through the emergency room." I looked at

Milt. "We can walk to the urgent care center later. It's just around the corner. Okay?"

Milt looked at Tony for assurance.

"It will probably be okay," Tony said. "As long as you get the elbow examined sooner rather than later." He looked sharply at me.

The paramedics finished checking my pulse and blood pressure, which was, understandably high. Milt and Tony spoke to the paramedics while I continued to adamantly refuse to be transported to the hospital.

Papers were signed, medical equipment was returned to the truck and the paramedics left.

Tony and Carol accompanied us back to our apartment, fussing over me nonstop. I now understood how Mrs. Pinsky must have felt when her daughter took her home from the hospital.

"Don't hesitate to call if you need anything." Carol said as she gave me a gentle hug. Milt shook hands with Tony and walked them to the door.

Neither one of us could speak, fearful of becoming emotionally unglued. My elbow was killing me. I went to the medicine cabinet in the bathroom to take Advil. I was waiting for the explosion from Milt, a reprimand for not paying attention when I crossed the street. I was certain that Milt believed the distraction was caused by my preoccupation with the murder, John's arrest and the missing Dudley brothers, which of course, it very well could have been.

The anticipated explosion never came. I walked into the kitchen. Milt was sitting with his head bent, cradled in his hands.

When he looked up, he was crying.

CHAPTER FOURTEEN

Seeing Milt in tears made me cry, and for the rest of the day we alternated between loving hugs and heated arguments, including a lot of 'I'm not' on my part, and 'Yes you are' on Milt's part.

The Advil eased the pain in my elbow, but Milt insisted on taking me to urgent care. I agreed, more for his sake than mine. An X-ray showed no break or fracture and we were reassured that the discomfort I felt would dissipate in time. Although I was still shaken by what had happened, I refused to think of the incident as anything more than the crazy and yes, almost lethal, stupidity of a driver, possibly drunk or high on something.

When Milt wasn't accusing me of not having paid attention while I had crossed the street, he was solicitous about how I was feeling, constantly asking if I needed anything. He took out the deli sandwiches he had bought and sat with me in the kitchen as we both ate in silence. I wasn't hungry, but I picked at the food to appease Milt's concern for my well being.

Once assured that I was indeed fine, he escaped to his workbench in the other bedroom to work on the dollhouse. I took a hot bath to help me relax and then tried to read in bed for a while. Not able to concentrate,

I got up and went to my desk. I reviewed what I had in my 'Sol Rubenstein' file and added notes from my visit to Helen's apartment, along with Bill and Carol's comments about John.

After a while, my mind wandered, making me question why I was even bothering anymore. Milt wanted me to stop interfering because he was worried about my safety. Andy wanted me to stop because he said it was a police investigation. Helen Brunner didn't appear to care one way or another. And, if being so preoccupied with the case was going to distract me when I crossed the street, well then maybe I should seriously consider closing down my personal investigation. I didn't actually make the commitment to stop, but I did put my files back in the drawer.

Milt had apparently decided to take a break from his wood working project, since he was asleep on the couch when I went in a while later to check on him. The TV was on and he had a book resting on his chest.

I don't know how long Milt was asleep, or what he did for dinner once he woke up. I returned to the bedroom, closed the drapes, and climbed into bed. Fighting visions of dead bodies, cars chasing me and dead ends, I pulled the covers over my head and eventually fell into a much needed sleep.

***

It was after eight when I woke up the next day. I couldn't recall the last time I had slept this long or this late. Milt wasn't in bed and for a moment, I panicked. He had been asleep on the couch when I went to bed.

Had he been there all night? Was he still mad at me? Was he all right?

I got out of bed, pulling on my robe as I made my way to the kitchen.

Milt had bread in the toaster, real eggs in the frying pan and fresh coffee brewing.

"You were out like a light last night," he said, pouring juice for me at the table. "I kept coming in to check on you, to make sure you were okay. You never heard me, huh?"

"No. Not a sound. I'm surprised I slept as well as I did." I wasn't sure how to gauge Milt's mood, however from all indications, I was optimistic.

"Well your body probably needed it." He poured coffee and placed a plate of toast and jam on the table. "How are you feeling?"

"My elbow still hurts a little when I move it, but I'll take more Advil. I'll be fine by the time we have to leave." I said. We had plans for this afternoon to attend a fundraising concert followed by dinner and dancing.

"Are you sure you're up to it?" Milt asked.

"Of course I'm up to it. It's just my elbow. And by the way, thank you for all this TLC. I could really get used to it."

Milt smiled and was about to say something when the phone rang. I answered on the first ring.

"Hi," our son's voice greeted me. "Everyone's fine," he assured me right away. "Susan and I wanted to see if you and Dad were up for a visit. We haven't seen you in a while so we thought we'd take the girls and come out this afternoon. That is, if you're available. I don't want you to change any plans you might have."

"We would love to have you and the family come for a visit Paul, and this afternoon would be wonderful." I looked at Milt who was nodding in agreement. "I'll pick up a turkey at the market. Or, would the girls would prefer something else, maybe pasta?"

"Whoa! Nothing doing, Mom." Paul said in a commanding voice. "We're taking you out for dinner. No arguments. Pick out a nice place. Make the reservation for five, five-thirty, if that's not too early for you and Dad."

"No. No, early works for us. But are you sure? I really don't mind having us stay here for dinner."

"I know you, Mom. If we eat at home you'll be jumping up and down every few seconds to wait on us. This way we can all relax and have a good visit.

"Okay. You win. It'll be so good to see you all. When do you think you'll be here?"

"Amanda had a birthday sleepover last night, so we have to pick her up, take her home and give her a chance to clean up. We should be able to get to you by around three. If it's later than that, I'll call."

"Sounds good. See you then."

"Well that's a nice surprise," I said as I hung up.

"What about the fundraiser?"

"It's okay," I said. "We'll send in a donation. I'd rather be with the kids."

"I agree," Milt said.

We finished breakfast and Milt, bless his heart, cleared the table and cleaned up the kitchen.

While the plan was to go out for dinner, I wanted to run out for some pretzels, crackers and cheese to have as a snack. Milt insisted that I stay home and he would go. I didn't argue and used the time to work on my Sol Rubenstein file. I was determined to find a common link to all the loose ends I seemed to have collected since Sol's murder. Deeply engrossed in rereading my notes, I didn't hear the knocking at first. When I did respond, I found Mrs. Pinsky standing at my door, looking pale and distraught.

"I was so worried," she said immediately. "I'm been knocking and knocking. Where were you? Everyone's talking about you being run over by a car. It's all over the building. Are you all right? Why didn't you go to the hospital? Where's your husband? Why are you alone? Sit down. You shouldn't be standing."

I waited for her to calm down and catch her breath. "I'm okay, Mrs. Pinsky. Come in." I held the door for her.

We sat in the kitchen. After assuring her that the car had not actually run over me, as apparently the rumors had indicated, she had me go over everything that had happened at the park. "Don't leave anything out," she directed. "Start with the moment you were crossing the street to when the car almost hit you."

So I did, although I tried to keep the drama at a minimum.

"Anyone get a license number?"

"Not that I know of. Frankly, I wasn't thinking straight at the time."

"I can imagine," she said, nodding slowly.

"What about you? How are you feeling?" I asked, turning the conversation around.

"Me? You mean because I fainted the other day? Pooh! That was nothing. Certainly not as exciting as what happened to you."

"Exciting? I wouldn't call nearly getting run over by someone who was either drunk, on drugs, or busy dialing his cell phone, exciting. Frightening, maybe, but not exciting. Oh, I almost forgot to ask you. Did you ever get a chance to bring kugel and chicken soup to Mr. Rubenstein?"

"I did." She answered shyly and I thought I detected a faint blush spreading across her face.

"You did? When? I mean you just got back yesterday morning."

"I made it after you and I spoke. I had all the ingredients, so it was no problem. I brought it to him last night."

"And…..?" I asked.

"And what? I brought it over, he took it, thanked me and said he'd return my plates in the morning." She was trying to appear blasé, but I saw right through her.

"And did he?"

"Yes."

She was beaming now. How cute was this, I thought.

"Good for you, Mrs. Pinsky. You did a good thing. Not only going to the funeral, but showing kindness by bringing him food. I'm sure he appreciates it."

"He's a very nice man. I don't know why I didn't notice him before. We got to talking this morning when he stopped by to return my plates."

"What did you talk about?" I was finding this quite amusing, although I was surprised at myself for not seeing the potential here a long time ago.

"Lots of things. Did you know he was a pharmacist before he retired? He worked for a large pharmacy in Manhattan."

"No, I didn't know that. What else did he have to say?"

"Nothing else….well, actually he told me he liked my cooking."

"Of course he likes your cooking. That's not a surprise." I laughed.

She smiled and stood up. "Well, if you're all right, Mrs. Maven, I've got to get back. I was very worried when I heard what had happened. I'm glad to see you're okay. Which elbow is it, by the way?"

"My left. Why?"

"I want to give you a hug but I don't want to hurt you." She leaned towards my right side, wrapping her arms gently around me, carefully avoiding the left side.

"Don't scare me like that again," she said with a smile. "It's not good for my heart!"

CHAPTER FIFTEEN

Milt returned carrying two large bags with snacks, juices, cans of soda and candy.

"Why'd you buy all this? I asked.

"For our guests." He answered, somewhat sheepishly.

"Right, for our guests."

After the bags were emptied and everything put away, we had a light lunch. "How did you like the par course, uh, I mean before the car attack?" Milt asked in between bites.

"It's a nice course, I just didn't have my heart in it." I said.

"How come?" Milt asked.

"I saw Carol Lucas there and once we started talking about John's arrest and how surprised she was, I couldn't concentrate on the workout."

Milt's entire body stiffened and I realized my mistake immediately. Shoot. I did it again. I shouldn't have said that.

"And that, I suppose, was what you were thinking about when you crossed the street without looking."

"Let's not even go there, Milt. Not now, okay? And please, let's not get our children all worked up by telling them about that either."

I walked out of the kitchen. I had been looking forward to the children's visit and didn't want anything to spoil it, especially Milt telling them about the car that almost killed me. I shuddered as I thought about it.

I went into the living room, sat down on the couch and picked up the newspaper.

A few minutes later the door bell rang. With the arrival of the family, our small hallway became a blur of hugs, kisses, coats, gloves and gift wrapped packages the girls kept insisting we open right then and there.

"Grandma, open up my present. I made this for you last night." Emily, our eight year old granddaughter said, pushing two large envelopes at us. One's for you and the other's for Papa."

"And wait till you see my present, Grandma." Amanda, who just turned eleven, was holding a small, neatly wrapped package in her outstretched hand. "I made it at the birthday party last night. I'm sorry I didn't make one for you Papa, but this was just for girls."

"That's okay sweetie," Milt said laughing. "I understand."

"Hold on, hold on, children." I said. Their enthusiasm and excitement was infectious and overwhelming. "Let's go into the living room. The light's better and we can sit down and open presents then."

Once settled in the living room, Amanda placed the package in my hand.

"Grandma, I made this just for you." She repeated. "I can't wait for you to see it. I hope, I hope you like it. I made it last night at my friend Jenny's house. Her mother hired an artist to come and teach us how to make jewelry."

"Jewelry? Wow." I said, opening the package as quickly as I could. Inside the box was a pair of drop earrings made from multi-colored crystals.

"Amanda, these are absolutely beautiful." I held the earrings up for everyone to see. "They look so professional. I'm very impressed that you made these." I gave her a hug.

Amanda was beaming. "Put them on, Grandma. I want to see how they look on you."

I removed the plain gold earrings I had been wearing and slipped the new ones on.

"Well? How do I look?" I turned my head from side to side for effect.

"Gorgeous," Milt offered.

"They go well with your coloring, Mom," Paul added.

"Very nice indeed," Susan said. "I knew you'd love them. Amanda's promised to make a pair for me."

"Now open mine, Grandma." Emily had been patiently waiting for her turn.

"I made something for you too, Papa." Emily's envelopes held large watercolor paintings, a sailboat for Milt and a rainbow for me.

After waxing poetic on the outstanding gifts of art and jewelry, Milt and I hugged both our granddaughters.

"This will go right up on our bedroom wall where all our other masterpieces are," Milt said as he went for the tape.

I drew both girls close to me for another thank you hug. In so doing, my head brushed against Emily and the right earring fell out.

"Oh dear. I hope I didn't do anything wrong." I looked around for the fallen piece of jewelry.

Amanda retrieved it. "No. See, Grandma, you didn't do anything wrong. I think it's the wire hook that holds the crystals. It needs to be rounded more. When you brushed against Emily it made the earring fall out. Maybe Papa can fix it."

"Let me take a look," Milt said as he returned to the living room. "Oh, this is easy to fix. I'll take care of it tomorrow."

"Well, I want to wear them today," I said, taking the earring back from Milt. "I'll just be extra careful not to brush against anything. I'll probably be checking my right ear a million times this evening." I chuckled as I touched my ear.

"That's okay, Grandma," Amanda said. Emily and I will keep an eye on your ear for you." We all laughed.

"Okay," Paul said. "The girls brought some games with them, so girls, why don't you go into the kitchen and play for a while. Mom and I want to talk to Grandma and Papa."

The girls did as they were told.

"Uh oh, this sounds ominous," I said, remembering Frannie's concerns when she and Julie came to visit.

"No, nothing ominous," Paul said. "Susan and I want to know what's going on. Frannie called me and said you were getting involved in this murder investigation and she's worried that it could become dangerous."

"Dangerous?" I said. "Nonsense. I'm only asking a few questions among the neighbors. And the police have apparently arrested the person who killed Sol, so there's not a lot left to become involved in."

"Humph, I think it's a bit more complicated than that," Milt grumbled.

"Milt...?"

"No, Sadie. I have to agree with our children." Milt said. "I've tried to be supportive, but you know how I feel about this. It's gotten out of hand and I'm really concerned."

"Concerned? What exactly are you concerned about, Milt?"

"I'm concerned that you have become completely absorbed by this. You don't sleep and almost every conversation revolves around the investigation. Besides, I'm not convinced that you weren't thinking of these things when that car almost hit you yesterday."

Oh boy! Here we go.

"What!" Paul was out of his seat. Susan's face had turned white."

"Paul, sit down, it was just some drunk driver. Your father is exaggerating." I gave Milt a stern look.

"No, I am absolutely not exaggerating. That car came this close to hitting you." He held up his thumb and index finger.

"Milt stop, please." I pleaded.

"You. Were. Almost. Hit. By. A. Car?" Paul's voice was strained.

Milt looked at me, then turned towards Paul and Susan. "Your mother was coming back from the park yesterday when a speeding car careened towards her. I saw it. I was on my way back from the photo copy place. If someone hadn't pushed her back to the curb, she'd be, well, I don't even want to think of that."

Milt faced me. "I know you say that since the police have John Brunner in custody, it's over and there's nothing more to worry about. But I know you and I don't think that's necessarily the whole picture. I'm certain that you were distracted by Sol's death and you weren't paying attention to the cars when you were crossing the street."

"I wasn't distracted." I said, trying desperately not to cry. The truth was that I had been distracted and I was ashamed that I had let that happen. I couldn't bring myself to admit that though, not to Milt and certainly not to my children.

"I think you were." Milt said. "You don't believe John Brunner is the right guy, and you're not willing to let the police figure it all out. You have this need to be right in the middle of everything and I'll be darned if I know why you feel that way."

"It's because I care." I stammered, probably sounding like a whiny kid. "It's because I was the one who told the police about John in the first place and if, just if, he's not guilty, then I feel a responsibility to find out what's going on."

"Like what?" Milt asked. "If the police feel they have a strong suspect, shouldn't that be enough to put this thing to rest? Don't you think they have a little bit more evidence to go on than your suspicions or intuition? Besides, what's left to poke around in, for heavens sake?"

Milt and I had become oblivious of Paul and Susan who were watching this exchange very closely. All the angst of the past few days were spilling out from both of us.

"The disappearance of the Dudley brothers, for one thing." I continued. "Maybe they were involved with John, or maybe John's innocent and it was Chuck and Pete Dudley all along. Then there's the strange turnaround in Helen Brunner's behavior less than twelve hours after her husband was arrested."

I was babbling now, trying to make everyone understand. I should have kept quiet when Milt brought up the car incident. I should have smiled sweetly and offered our children something to eat. But I didn't. I kept explaining and defending, hating this feeling of having to justify my actions.

"I don't know what's going on with Helen Brunner, but something about her doesn't sit well with me. As for the police having a strong suspect, you're right, I'm not so sure. Andy's not talking and there's been no update as to what evidence they have on John. I mean, sure he made threatening remarks and then has no strong alibi for the time period, but I'll bet that's true of a lot of people in this building, including the Dudley boys."

The silence in the room was deafening.

Paul and Susan exchanged worried glances.

"Uh, Mom, this is exactly what we were afraid of." Paul spoke in a soft and gentle voice. "You know this is serious stuff here. You really shouldn't be personally interfering in a murder investigation no matter how good your intentions might be."

"But I'm...."

"Sorry Mom, but what you're doing is risky. You're interfering with police work, stepping on innocent people's toes, tampering with an ongoing investigation, all of which could result in fines or worse, jail, personal injury and possibly endangering others."

"Oh, Paul, really! Isn't that a bit melodramatic?"

I was mad at myself for letting the visit get so out of hand. I folded my arms over my chest, tightened my lips, drew in a breath and as much as a person can actually accomplish this, I fumed.

Then I saw Paul's expression. He looked hurt and I immediately felt guilty. Of course, I realized sadly, isn't that what mothers do best? I couldn't even have a moment of fuming without feeling badly for the effect it had on others.

"I'm sorry Paul. I know you have my best interests at heart, but don't you think this is making a big deal out of nothing?"

"No. Not at all. There is considerable risk in continuing what you're doing."

"You really could get hurt," Susan added kindly. "We know you mean well, but we, all of us, do not want you to get into something that could potentially cause you any harm."

"Okay. Okay." I threw my hands up in the air. "I give up."

"You mean you'll finally stop your meddling and persistent interfering?" Milt asked with apparent skepticism.

"It's not meddling, Milt!" I shouted. Then I looked at my loved ones standing in front of me. They had such long faces I didn't know whether to laugh or cry. In spite of my anger, I couldn't go on arguing my point over and over. It wouldn't make any difference anyway. I took a deep breath. I smiled, hoping to make my words sound light, but determined. "I'm not making any promises. However, I'll try to keep my persistent involvement low key and, hopefully, not cause my family any more anxiety or stress."

Milt sighed, shaking his head.

Paul and Susan exchanged glances again, but then Paul, bless his heart, must have decided they had pushed me as far as I would go.

"Fair enough," Paul said, standing up. "Now where are we going for dinner? I don't know about anyone else, but I'm starved!"

Ah! Thank you Paul. We now had a truce, a pause, and a brief respite from my ongoing saga.

If only that had lasted.

CHAPTER SIXTEEN

Grateful for having moved beyond the drama of the moment, we nodded in agreement with Paul.

"I made reservations at a terrific new Italian restaurant not too far from here." I said, retrieving coats, jackets and scarves for everyone as we got ready to leave. "We haven't eaten there yet, but our friends raved about the food, so I thought we'd give it a try."

The Italian restaurant was on Ocean Parkway, a twenty-minute drive from the apartment building. We all fit into Paul's new SUV, admiring the elaborate sound system, video player attachment, cup holders, magazine pockets, individual climate control buttons and every other state of the art device that could be built into the interior of the car.

My new earring had fallen out again as I was putting on my coat. I had been tempted to leave the earrings behind until Milt was able to fix it, but I wanted Amanda to know how much I liked what she had made. I insisted on wearing the earrings, hoping I wouldn't regret my decision.

We found a parking spot a block away and enjoyed the easy stroll to the restaurant.

I walked ahead with Susan and the girls. The girls kept vying for my attention with their various stories about school, their favorite books, their friends and their after school activities.

Milt and Paul lagged behind us, talking sports. Apparently there had been some exciting finish to one of the basketball games, because Milt suddenly called out for us to 'hang on a second.'

"What is it?" I asked as we stopped and looked back at them.

Milt was reaching into his pocket for change. "I want to buy the evening newspaper." He approached the newsstand a few feet away from the restaurant, inserted the coins and pulled out a copy.

He found the sports section, hurried over to the light near the entrance and handed me the rest of the papers as he searched for the relevant sports story. In the process, the local section of the newspaper fell out. As I bent down to retrieve it, my eyes caught a headline over an accompanying photo of Chuck and Pete Dudley.

"Oh my goodness, look at this." I said moving towards the light and reading aloud.

> *"Brothers Found Safe In Utah.*
>
> *A search for Chuck and Pete Dudley, ended on a positive note early this morning when the two brothers walked into a police station in Utah. The police had been looking for them since last Wednesday when Sol Rubenstein, the owner of the apartment building where they lived, was found murdered following a heated tenant meeting.*
>
> *After police questioned several tenants, they learned that the brothers had made threatening remarks to Mr. Rubenstein*

*during the meeting and then apparently dis-
appeared soon after.*

*While the police insisted the two men
were not suspects in the case, they did affirm
that they were interested in questioning them
about any information they might have had
regarding the events of that evening.*

*According to the police, the two men had
left for Utah immediately after the meeting.
The men, unemployed at the time, said they
had been offered a construction job in Utah
and had to be there by the end of the week.
They told the police that they had left the
apartment building around ten o'clock that
evening, driving straight through to Utah.
After verifying their story, the two men were
released.*

*According to Andy Cohen, homicide
detective with the Brooklyn police department, the discovery of the Dudley brothers was
good news. "We're very pleased to learn that
their whereabouts have been established, and
that they were not harmed."*

*Detective Cohen would not comment on
the ongoing murder investigation of apartment building owner Sol Rubenstein, or the
arrest of John Brunner as a suspect in case."*

I finished reading and looked up to see my family
patiently giving me their full attention. Even the grandchildren, sensing something going on, had been merci-
fully quiet and patient.

I must have looked somewhat distraught, because Paul walked over and put his arm around me. "Mom, you've got to stop taking this whole thing so personally. This is what I was talking about. You're getting yourself worked up over the investigation and everyone involved in it. It's taken over your life."

"Paul, don't be silly. I just read a small article from the newspaper that I found particularly interesting. It's nothing more than what you and Dad do when you read an article on sports."

"Well then." Milt said anxiously. "At least this information should put a cap on all your doubts about the Dudleys. They've been found. They're safe. Now you can stop worrying about them. Right?" He looked hopefully at me.

Not wanting to rekindle the uncomfortable discussion from before, I smiled, nodded, and walked ahead into the restaurant.

But truth be told, the cap, as Milt put it, was still miles away from being put on anything, let alone anywhere near my growing doubts about the case and the individuals involved.

CHAPTER SEVENTEEN

I was good. I pretended that the news regarding the Dudley brothers was of no further interest or concern. While I was dying to talk about the article and get feedback on its importance, I kept my thoughts, my actions and my deeds, in careful check the whole evening. As we waited for our dinner, I played tic tac toe on scraps of paper with Amanda and Emily and made them laugh with my attempt to recall a few knock-knock jokes. I listened to everyone's stories, asked questions about work and school, and basically tried to keep the conversation focused on Paul, Susan and the girls.

It helped that the restaurant was crowded, the noise deafening and the food terrific. We were ravenous when we were finally seated and, as a result, over ordered and over ate. We wound up having the server pack up the remaining lasagna, cheese ravioli and home made bread for us to take home.

When dinner was over, we walked leisurely back to the car. The fresh air felt good and all in all, we were satiated and relaxed when the kids dropped us off in front of the apartment building. After kisses and hugs and reassurances that we would take care of ourselves, Milt and I went upstairs.

It was a little after eight o'clock when we walked in. Too early for the news, but I was anxious anyway. I wanted to see if there were any updates on the Dudley brothers.

Milt had gone into the living room immediately after walking in. He sat down on the recliner and reached for the remote.

After refrigerating the leftovers and checking messages, I went into the bedroom and changed into comfortable, stay-at-home-nobody-will see-me-except-Milt clothes. My elbow still hurt, but not as much.

I went into the kitchen, made tea for myself and sat down to read the rest of the newspapers. I was tired, but I wanted to stay up for the news.

When I walked into the living room sometime later, Milt was watching a sitcom. I closed my eyes for what I thought would be a few minutes. Apparently I had been more tired than I thought, because I dozed for some time, awakening to the TV anchorwoman's voice announcing the upcoming news stories.

The news regarding the Dudley brothers and the murder investigation was a recap with basically the same information I'd read in the newspaper. The only new insight was some speculation that John Brunner might not have been the murderer after all. According to the anchorwoman, although the police had not actually come out and said as much, someone involved in the investigation had let it slip, off the record, and it was now being checked out.

I perked up at that bit of news, wondering if it was true and if so, what would happen next.

When the phone rang a little after ten, I went into the kitchen to answer it. I was thinking that it might have been the kids.

"Hello." There was no response. "Hello? Hello?" I hung up.

"Who was that?" Milt called out from the living room.

"No one was there. Probably a wrong number."

The phone rang again.

"Hello."

I heard a low, almost muffled male voice. "You were lucky yesterday. I won't miss a second time. If you know what's good for you, you'll keep your nose out of the John Brunner investigation."

"Who is this?" I said with alarm.

Milt came into the kitchen.

The voice continued. "It doesn't matter who this is, just pay attention to what I said and mind your own business." The line went dead.

"What was that all about?" Milt asked. "You're white as a sheet."

"Some man told me to stop investigating the murder." I repeated in a shaky voice.

"Did you recognize the voice?" Milt was clearly agitated.

"No. It was muffled, like he had something covering the mouthpiece."

"We have to call the police." Milt said.

"Call and tell them what? That I got a threatening call from someone I don't know or even have the slightest idea who it could be?" I was frightened, but not smart enough to realize how dangerous this situation had become.

"Sadie. This phone call clearly means that yesterday's car thing wasn't a random act by someone drunk or on drugs. Someone was trying to kill you. You might not want to bother the police, but I sure as hell have no qualms about doing just that." He picked up the phone and dialed.

I sat down, too stunned to think. Someone wanted to kill me? Because I was asking questions and he didn't like that? This was ridiculous. It had to be a prank.

Your friend, Detective Cohen, wasn't in." Milt told me after replacing the phone. "The person I spoke to took down all the information. He said the police will check it out. This settles it."

"Settles what?"

"No more involvement with the police investigation. I'm serious about this, Sadie. Your entire family has been uncomfortable with your personal interference with this from the beginning. Now this clenches it."

"But Milt, don't you see? If someone is making this call, it's because he's afraid I might uncover something that could point the finger of guilt away from John and back to him, whoever he is. Even the news this evening reported some speculation that John might not be guilty."

"No buts, Sadie. Whoever has our number knows who you are and where you live. This affects all of us. What if he really does want to hurt you, not just scare you? What if Julie's here when he attempts another attack? Or one of the other grandchildren? You have to take this seriously."

"You're right, of course. And I do take it seriously. It's just that I was hoping it was a prank call." I said weakly.

"This was no prank."

"I know." That reality was hitting me hard. I didn't want anything to happen to anyone, including myself.

"Do you have any idea what you put me through? Seeing you almost get hit by a speeding car coming right at you." Milt shuddered. "It was my worst nightmare."

"I'm sorry." I said meekly as Milt put his hand on my shoulder.

"It's over. No more questions. No more interfering with the police investigation. No more personal involvement." He said.

I nodded and slowly walked into the bedroom. I sat down heavily on the bed. There was still so much about the murder that needed to be sorted out, but I was done. The horrible vision of the car careening towards me yesterday, and the threatening phone call today, had done the job. I was scared. I was also tired of this whole business, the unanswered questions, the family interventions and concerns, the friction it had caused in our marriage and the frustration of not being able to do anything about any of it. I was ready to let go of it all.

The question, of course, was why I didn't.

CHAPTER EIGHTEEN

Neither of us slept that night. I was certain that every sound I heard was the guy who had made the threatening call. My imagination had him sneaking into the apartment, lurking in the dark, determined to find me. Milt couldn't sleep either. He said it was out of fear that I wouldn't keep my word and would somehow get back to what he called my 'P.I.' mission.

We both woke up tired and grumpy. When I mentioned how freaked out I was, Milt had little sympathy. "I know you're frightened and upset and that's good. As long as you're frightened, you won't do anything foolish."

He wasn't helping. I took a shower and got dressed. When I walked into the kitchen, Milt had coffee waiting for me.

"Thanks." I said, taking a sip. "Don't you have an appointment with the accountant today?" It would be good for him to go, to do his own thing and for us to have some space. I was upset enough and certainly not in the mood for any more lectures from Milt.

"Yes, at eleven. I'll leave the house around ten, just to give me extra time in case the trains are late. I should be home around one."

I nodded.

"Are you mad at me?" Milt asked.

"No. Just unsettled."

He kissed me lightly on the cheek before going into the bedroom to get ready for his appointment. I had some cereal, finished my coffee and cleaned up the kitchen.

After Milt left for his appointment, I called Andy. I didn't want Milt listening in while I repeated all the details of the car scene and the phone call. Plus, Milt would probably stand right next to me, coaching me as to what I should say to Andy. I didn't need that.

The person who took my call informed me that Andy was not in at the moment but that she would be happy to take a message. I told her that it was important and asked if she could please let Andy know that I had called.

I didn't know what to do with myself when I hung up. I didn't want to miss Andy's call, however, I didn't want to wait by the phone all day either. The threatening caller had left his mark. I was scared and out of sorts. I needed something to do. I had a good three hours or so until Milt returned and decided this would be a good time to pay another visit to Mr. Rubenstein. I felt guilty that I hadn't checked in on him earlier, but it never seemed to be the right moment.

In spite of my trepidation, I walked down the stairs to the first floor. The stairs still brought back vivid images of the murder scene, but I knew I had to get past that.

I didn't have to wait long after knocking on Mr. Rubenstein's door. "Come in." He opened the door wide.

I thought Mr. Rubenstein actually looked pleased to see me. Maybe our help with the Rabbi, the funeral and the *minyan*, had softened him up a little. Maybe it was Mrs. Pinsky's kugel. Or maybe he was just a lonely old man who didn't know how to reach out to others and was happy to have someone stop by.

"Is this a good time? I don't want to bother you, Mr. Rubenstein."

"Time is time." He answered. "At my age, what difference does it make?"

"Come." He said as I followed him to the kitchen. He pulled out a chair, removed the newspapers that had accumulated on top, and motioned for me to sit.

"I heard about the car thing. You okay?" He asked.

"Yes, thanks." I answered, instinctively touching my elbow. "There was no break or sprain. It's getting better." I chose not to tell him about the caller and the connection to the attack.

"How are you doing?" I asked.

"I'm doing. That's it." He went to the stove where a teapot had been warming. "I'm going to have a cup of tea. Would you like to join me?"

"That sounds good." I watched him take a box of Tetley tea and a small cup filled with sugar cubes from his cupboard. He filled two cups with hot water and sat down across from me.

"Mr. Rubenstein," I hesitated, stirring a sugar cube into my tea. "Would you mind if I ask you a question? It's about your son and his, um, death." I told myself this question was out of pure interest. It had absolutely nothing to do with any personal involvement, which I had promised Milt I would no longer be pursuing.

"Ask." He said.

"Was your son with you that evening before he was mur…, I mean, before, you know, he was killed?"

"Yes." He stared at his cup for a moment. "Solly came here a little after eight that evening. He told me the meeting was a disaster. He was upset over how badly it went, saying he hadn't realized how angry everyone was over the pending sale."

"You mean he actually didn't understand how much of an impact the sale would have on the tenants? I told Sol about the neighbors being upset and angry, when I first spoke to him that afternoon. That's why I hoped he'd come to talk to them."

"I know. He mentioned your call, but I think he felt you were exaggerating. He just couldn't believe it was as bad as you described it." Mr. Rubenstein set down his cup. "You see, my Solly was a good man. He saw this as a business transaction. He didn't mean it as anything personal. He just didn't see it from their perspective."

I nodded sadly.

"Did Sol do or say anything else while he was here?" I asked, still out of pure interest of course.

"No. We had tea. He took care of my bills. He asked if I needed anything and when I said no, that I was fine, he got up, put away his cup and saucer, and said goodbye."

"Did your son get any phone calls while he was here?"

"As a matter of fact he did. He got a call on his cell phone just before he left."

My heart skipped a beat. "Do you know who called him?"

"No. I heard Solly tell whoever was on the phone that he'd be there in a few minutes. Then he hung up. I didn't ask Solly about his business. If he wanted me to know something, he'd tell me. He said goodbye again and left."

"Do the police know that he spoke to someone that evening?"

"Yes. The police asked me the same question. I told them what I told you."

I mentally filed that piece of information away for a later conversation with Andy, feeling myself drifting deeper and deeper into this personal intrigue all over again. Promise, what promise?

"Okay." I was now all fired up. "What time did your son leave that night?"

"Maybe a little before nine o'clock, give or take a minute or two."

I drank my tea, trying to put the pieces together. If Sol was called away at nine, and his body was found approximately a half hour later, he could not have gone far.

"Do you think the call came from someone in the building? Someone who convinced him of the importance of going upstairs to one of the apartments?"

"It's possible." Mr. Rubenstein answered.

"If that's the case," I continued. "Then Sol would have had to have been somehow dragged to the stairs and thrown over. He could have been drugged, but there hasn't been any mention of that in the news."

Fortunately I came to my senses at this point and stopped voicing the rest of my glory thoughts out loud. What I almost said, in my ramblings, was that additional newspaper reports had indicated that there had been a blow to Sol's head and the police were awaiting test results to determine if the blow was caused by the fall or from a blunt object prior to the fall. Way too much information for Sol's father to hear.

"Yoo hoo. Mrs. Maven. You all right?" Mr. Rubenstein waved his hands in front of me. He had obviously been talking, but I had mentally spaced out.

"I'm so sorry, Mr. Rubenstein. I was trying to assimilate this new information and make some sense out of it."

"Why?" He asked.

"Why?" I laughed aloud. "That's a question that's been asked of me a lot lately."

"Nu? So again, why?" He said. "And, as for making sense, there's no sense in murder."

"No, of course not. What I'm trying to make sense out of is John Brunner's part in all this. For what it's worth, I don't think he did it. I think someone else killed your son."

Mr. Rubenstein remained silent.

"I'm so sorry, Mr. Rubenstein." I said. "I really shouldn't be talking to you about any of this. You have enough sorrow without adding my two cents to it."

"No, no. That's okay," he patted my hand. "Actually I was considering pretty much the same thing. Now that you put that into words I see that it's possible. I didn't think the call had anything to do with Solly's murder at first, but you're right. Whoever called him was trying to get him to go someplace. Probably up to one of the apartments."

"Yes, that's exactly what I've been thinking." I was excited. This was the first time in the investigation that anyone had even remotely followed my line of reasoning, let alone agreed with it.

"Did Sol give out his cell phone number to many people?"

"Solly lived on the phone. He was always expecting important calls, so yes, I guess he did. Besides, he had business cards with his cell phone number. And anyone calling his office could get his number as well. Oh, and his secretary, of course. And now that I think of it, his voice mail gave out the number too."

"Well, so much for that." I felt disappointed. With so many people having access to his cell phone number, it would have been impossible to guess who might have called him that night.

"I wonder if the police were able to trace the origin of the phone call." I said thinking that I'd ask Andy about the trace if and when I finally got through to him. Unfortunately, once I told him about the car and the threatening phone call, I was pretty sure I wouldn't get Andy to tell me anything other than, stay out of this. And that, I'd already heard from Milt.

We sat quietly for a few minutes considering what we had discussed.

"Do you have any idea who it could have been? The killer, I mean." Mr. Rubenstein asked quietly.

"No. But if it was one of the neighbors, it would have to be someone on one of the higher floors, maybe fourth, fifth or sixth."

Actually even the second or third could be deadly, I thought, trying to calculate how many apartments that would involve if I wanted to personally interview each tenant.

"If my math is right, each floor has four apartments on each side of the stairs." I said. "If we just count the third through sixth floors, that adds up to 32 apartments, 64 adults, give or take a few vacancies, single occupancies, and individuals who might not have been home that evening."

Mr. Rubenstein nodded, but remained quiet.

"That's a lot of people who could have made that call." I slumped back in my chair as the futility of the situation hit me.

"You know," Mr. Rubenstein said in a quiet voice. "I can get you a list of all the apartments, the ones that are rented and the ones that are vacant. Would that help?"

I perked up immediately. "That would be very helpful. But are you sure you're okay with this?"

"Mrs. Maven, nothing would give me more satisfaction than being able to help catch Solly's killer. If you think it will help, then I'll call the office right now and get Nancy, Solly's assistant, to look up the information."

"Yes, it would certainly narrow down the number of people in this building who could have made that call."

"Then I'll do it. If the police are certain they have the killer, they aren't going to go after anyone else. I didn't really know John Brunner, but I can't see what his reason would have been to hurt my Solly."

"You don't think the selling of the building made him angry enough to do it?"

"People were upset about the sale, but killing Solly doesn't mean the problem's solved. Solly left the building to me in the event of his demise," Mr. Rubenstein stated firmly. "As far as I know, he didn't change his will, so that still stands. And the final sale wasn't going to take place till the end of the month."

"I had no idea."

"No one knew except Sabrina and she was never happy about Solly's decision to leave the building to me," he smiled mischievously.

"So as far as the tenants are concerned, Solly's death put a temporary halt to the proceedings. That said, the tenants had to at least assume, that since the property was being run by his company, the deal would ultimately go through, with or without him."

"Is that what will happen?" I asked.

"No."

"No?"

"No." Mr. Rubenstein said. "I always thought Solly was making a mistake selling this building. I told him a couple of times, but he said it was a business decision and that I shouldn't worry. He said I'd be taken care of one way or another."

"Meaning financially?"

"Yes, that too. But Solly had it written into the contract, regarding this building, that if he were to die before the sale, the building would go to me. Any negotiations to buy the property would have to be started over again with me. Also, if I did agree to sell, it was on the condition that I was to stay on indefinitely as long as that was what I wanted to do."

"So what happens now?" I asked. "You said the building won't be sold."

"That's right. I don't want to sell the building and now that it's going to legally be mine, I don't have to."

Michelle Gabriel

"But I thought you said that since the property was being run by your son's company, the deal would ultimately go through, with or without him." I had obviously missed a beat here.

"Not necessarily. The deal has understandably been put on hold but once the estate is cleared and all the paperwork is taken care of, I'll be the official owner. Then I'll meet with the people who want to buy the building and tell them it's no longer for sale."

"I'm sure they won't be happy about that." I said.

"No. Probably not. But these things happen a lot in business. There'll be a penalty that I'll have to pay or some sort of monetary settlement, but they can't force me to sell, so that will be that."

"I'm amazed. I really had no idea."

"I know." He said. "But now that you do, please don't tell anyone. Not yet, anyway. I want to wait until the police investigation is over. When this whole mess is resolved and Solly's killer is put away, then I'll concentrate on the building."

"I understand. I won't say a word." I walked over and gave him a hug. "You know Mr. Rubenstein, you're going to make a lot of people very happy with your announcement."

He shrugged, but I noticed the beginnings of a smile.

"By the way," I asked. "How is Sabrina taking all this, the fact that you're not going to sell the building?"

He laughed out loud for the first time. "It's a moot point."

"What do you mean?"

"Solly treated Sabrina like royalty, giving in to just about all her demands, but he drew the line when it came to the business. She fought him on that, wanting to have the business go to her if anything happened, but Solly had her sign one of those, what do you call, before the wedding contracts."

"A prenuptial?"

"Yeah, that's what it was, a prenuptial. So she couldn't touch his business under any circumstances. But don't feel sorry for her, she gets a bundle of money along with the expensive jewelry, clothes and the Manhattan condo. She won't go hungry."

"So you wind up in the real estate business?" I asked kindly.

"Well, yes, sort of. My Solly was an only child. He didn't have partners and didn't trust anyone else to run his business. Even with the corporation, it was still Solly who made all the decisions. He pretty much left the paperwork to the corporation lawyers and accountants, but he always had the final say."

"Your son owned more than this building, right?"

"Yes. Technically, he left the entire business to me, all of his property. However, knowing that I wasn't about to start running it at my age, he also made provisions in his will, to sell all of his holdings except this apartment building, which he left to me. A generous percentage of the total amount received from the sale of the other property will also be left for me. The rest of the proceeds, a very nice sum I might add, will go to cancer research. Surprised, huh?"

"Yes, frankly I am. To be honest with you, and I mean no disrespect, but Solly, I mean Sol, didn't seem that, uh, compassionate at the meeting." I just couldn't mesh the Sol his father just described, with the image of Sol I saw at the meeting, abruptly dismissing our questions and concerns.

"I know," Mr. Rubenstein agreed. "Solly could be that way sometimes. When it came to running the business, he was a tough one. That's why I stayed away from that part of his life. When he visited, we talked about anything but the business."

"I'm sorry," I said again. "I shouldn't have said what I said.

"No." He said. "You're right. I can see how you would have seen only that side of him. But he had a good heart, my Solly."

"One more question." I said. "If you now own this building, how will you run it? I mean, it's a lot of work. Can you do it on your own?"

"A better question would be, do I want to do it on my own? The answer is no. I know my limitations. I've been in touch with my nephew, my sister's oldest son. He's in real estate in California and he's coming to see me next month. We'll talk. We'll see what we can work out. For now, Nancy can hold down the fort and take care of things."

My tea had gotten cold, but it didn't matter. I now had a whole bunch of other information to ponder.

"Okay," I said, trying to recollect my thoughts. "I guess that rules out money as a motive. So the question remains, why would anyone want to kill Sol?"

"That, Mrs. Maven, is a question I have been trying to answer ever since he died. He was a good man. A good son and a good husband. He probably made a lot of people unhappy with his business decisions, but I can't believe that would have been enough of a reason to kill him. But who knows, it could have been some crazy person who just felt like killing someone."

He looked off into space. I remained quiet. Suddenly he got up and went for the phone.

"I'll call Nancy and get that information for you."

He spoke for a few minutes before disconnecting. "She wants to help in any way she can," he said. She said she'd access the files and bring the papers here this evening after work."

"Great! Would you mind if I dropped in again this evening, around eight or so, to see the information?"

"Of course I won't mind," he said with a smile. "I'd be disappointed if you didn't."

CHAPTER NINETEEN

I left Mr. Rubenstein's apartment feeling charged with new energy. Milt was not going to be happy that I was getting involved with any of this again, but my visit had given me new resolve. I wanted, no, I needed to be a part of this investigation. I had to feel that I was being helpful and an active participant within my little universe of family, friends and neighbors. Sitting by the sidelines was not an option I had ever taken and I was not about to start doing that now.

I was convinced that John Brunner was not the killer. Once I had the list of tenants, I was pretty sure I'd have something tangible to work with to confirm that belief. At the very least, I thought I'd be able to narrow the number of suspects by eliminating any unlikely ones, such as the elderly, the sick or those not home during the evening of the murder. It was a stretch, but it was something.

On a whim, I decided to go to the library to let Helen Brunner know about my suspicions, now seconded by Mr. Rubenstein, of her husband's innocence. In spite of what I perceived to be her indifference to my involvement and her weird behavior the other day, I hoped she'd at least be pleased to hear my thoughts.

The weather was on the cool side, brisk, but sunny. It felt good to walk, although I remained on high alert as I crossed the streets. Still, I was happy being proactive again. Maybe I'd even be able to help speed up John Brunner's release.

The walk to the library took less than twenty minutes. I didn't see Helen Brunner at first, so I wandered over to the young adult section. Amanda and Emily had been talking about the Harry Potter books the other night. This would be a good opportunity to check out the book and see what all the fuss was about.

There were several copies on the shelf. I selected J.K. Rowling's *Harry Potter and The Sorcerer's Stone*, as well as her second book, *Harry Potter and the Chamber of Secrets.*

That done, I walked over to the adult area. Helen Brunner was stacking books on a shelf behind her desk.

I stopped behind one of the bookshelves nearby. Hidden from view, I watched her undetected.

She was wearing an attractive looking navy blue pantsuit with a light beige blouse. Her makeup highlighted her features, which up to recently had been almost nondescript. With her curly hair and fashionable clothes, she looked years younger. In fact she looked fantastic, not unlike the way she had looked when I saw her on Saturday.

After finishing her task, Helen walked around her desk in my direction.

I walked ahead, pretending to be deep in concentration as I read the jacket on one of the Harry Potter books in my hand. As I continued walking, head down, I bumped right into her.

"Oops, sorry. Oh! Hi there, Mrs. Brunner. I forgot you work here on Monday mornings." Okay, I told a little fib, but I couldn't come right out and tell her that I came just to see her.

"I picked up a few books." I held them up for her to see.

"Harry Potter?"

"My granddaughters have been raving about the books." I explained truthfully. "I promised them I'd read at least the first two in the series so we could share our thoughts about Muggles, Quidditch and The Forbidden Forrest."

She smiled politely and was about to excuse herself, when I jumped in again.

"Did you have a nice visit with your friend on Saturday?"

She stared at me blankly for a few seconds. "Oh, Saturday. Right. Yes, thank you. We had a very nice visit."

"Good. And how is your husband doing, I mean, is he being treated well, is he all right with the attorney they've assigned to him?"

"Uh, John's fine, I suppose. I don't know if they're assigned an attorney to him or not." Helen seemed distracted. "He's still insisting that he didn't do anything wrong. The police are trying to get him to confess, telling him that it would go easier for him if he does. I think so too. I've told him that, but he's very angry and won't listen to anything I say."

"Well Mrs. Brunner, I think John's situation is going to change very soon."

"What do you mean?"

"I heard on the news last night that the police are no longer sure they arrested the right person."

"Really? I haven't heard anything about that." Her voice sounded strained.

"This has to be so difficult for both of you." I continued talking, hoping to break through her stony demeanor. "I'm really so sorry."

She nodded, but remained quiet. She looked at her watch. "You'll have to excuse me, Mrs. Maven, I have to get back to work. Goodbye." She turned and quickly walked away.

"Mrs. Brunner," I called after her, hurrying to catch up. "I just have one question I'd like to ask you, if you don't mind. I'll make it quick."

"What is it?" She looked irritated.

"Mr. Rubenstein said Sol received a call that evening, on his cell phone. It was right after the tenant meeting. Do you know if your husband called him?"

"No. I don't know if John called Sol Rubenstein. John had gone out that night, right after we got back from the meeting, remember? I told you about that. What makes you think I would know who had called Sol Rubenstein?"

"I'm just trying to follow up on that information. We think it might have been someone in the apartment building who made the call."

"You think, Mrs. Maven? You and Mr. Rubenstein? Well, I for one, think you should just mind your own business. Now, you really must let me get back to my work. Goodbye."

Whoa! Talk about abrupt. This woman switched moods more often than some women switched purses.

I stared at her as she walked away. Mind my own business? I couldn't imagine what that was all about.

And to think, just last week she couldn't thank me enough for my help!

CHAPTER TWENTY

I didn't know what to make of Helen Brunner. As I walked home I kept thinking of her strange behavior. First she was cold and abrupt, then all sweet and kind, apologizing for her previous behavior. Then she was back to her cold self when I visited her in the apartment, and then again today. She didn't even seem that interested in the possibility of her husband's innocence. Come to think of it, I had probably shown more excitement about that than she had.

Milt had not come back by the time I returned home. I found a message on our machine that Frannie had called. When I dialed her number, her machine picked up. I left a brief message for her before placing another call to Andy. He wasn't in either and I began to wonder if my calls to Andy weren't being put through anymore.

I sat down, intending to read Harry Potter when the phone rang.

I was relieved to hear Andy's voice. Maybe I wasn't on his, 'don't put her calls through to me' list, yet.

"Hello Mrs. Maven. How are you?"

"Fine, sort of." I said, trying to minimize the seriousness of what I was about to tell him. Part denial on my part, along with a strong dose of stupidity thrown into the mix.

"Sort of? What do you mean?"

"Well, Andy, I need to fill you in on a few things that have happened.

"Oh?"

"Yes." I said, clearing my throat and taking a deep breath. "Saturday afternoon I was coming back from the park. You know, the one right across the street from our apartment house?"

"Yes, I know the park." Andy's voice sounded guarded.

"I was about to cross the street when a car raced towards me. It would have hit me, but thankfully, someone saw what was happening and pushed me back just in time. My immediate thought had been that this was some idiot driver, distracted by a cell phone, or maybe high on drugs or alcohol. Then something happened yesterday and, well now I know it wasn't an accident." I shuddered, conjuring up all sorts of ugly and frightening images.

"What happened yesterday to make you believe that it wasn't an accident?"

"I had a threatening call."

"What do you mean, threatening call, Mrs. Maven?"

"Last night, sometime after ten, the phone rang. When I answered it, there was no one there, so I hung up. A few seconds later it rang again. This time when I picked up, a man's voice, it sounded muffled, told me to stop investigating the murder. He said I had been lucky yesterday and he wouldn't miss a second time. Then he told me to keep my nose out of the John

150

Brunner's investigation or someone was going to get hurt."

"Why didn't you call me as soon as you got the call?"

"I did, or rather Milt did. I was too bewildered. I was trying to convince myself that it had been some kind of a prank call. Milt said he left a message to call back."

"I never got that message." Andy said. I could hear papers being shuffled. "I only have your call from earlier today. What about the car incident? Did you report that?"

"No. Because, as I said, at the time I thought it was some nut on the road. No one got a license and the car, well, it was a basic dark colored sedan and I never got a look at the driver, although I do remember from that split second look, seeing just one person in the car."

"We take all threatening phone calls seriously, Mrs. Maven." Andy said. "And now the call, on top of the fact that someone wanted to scare you off by trying to run you down, obviously means you've been asking too many questions about the murder. That's most likely getting someone nervous. We'll trace the phone call of course, but meanwhile, I hope you're not continuing to snoop around anymore."

I didn't answer at first. Then I decided to just blurt it all out.

"First of all, Andy, I don't consider my asking questions to be a matter of snooping. The car and the call frightened me very much. Milt went ballistic and like you, told me to stop interfering. I agreed to do that, for a while, but then I spoke to Mr. Rubenstein and he told me some interesting information which makes me question motive, opportunity, location and a bunch of other related issues."

"Mrs. Maven, do you realize you're putting yourself in a very dangerous situation? You could also be endangering your husband and other members of your family. Right now whoever is behind this is just trying to scare you off. I'm sure of that, or we wouldn't be having this conversation. You'd be dead." Andy let that sink in a moment before continuing. "If you insist on doing this, I could arrest you, you know, for interfering with a police investigation."

"What? Andy, you can't be serious." I couldn't believe this kid, this boy I taught in religious school, would even consider putting me in jail. And I know his mother!

"I certainly hope it doesn't get to that point, however, I want you to understand how serious this is. The very fact that you are going around asking questions puts you at risk and could jeopardize our case."

"But what if I have information that helps your investigation?"

A deep sigh. "That's a different issue," Andy said, obviously struggling to stay calm. "Do you?"

"Yes, I do. But I wouldn't have any information, if I didn't ask questions." Now I was exasperated.

"What is your information?" His voice was quiet and tense. I could only imagine the great effort it must have taken him to keep his emotions under control.

"Morris Rubenstein told me that Sol received a call on his cell phone the night he was murdered. He also told me that you already knew that."

"That's correct. Go on."

"Because of that information, Mr. Rubenstein asked Sol's office assistant to bring over a list of all the apartments in the building to see which are rented and which are vacant. We're both fairly certain that who-ever made the phone call had to have been someone in the building that night."

Silence.

"We're going to check it out." I continued, enthused with my own belief that this was a monu-mental piece of news. "Nancy, Sol Rubenstein's assist-ant, is bringing the information to Mr. Rubenstein's apartment this evening. I'll be there then so we can review it together. Now tell me Andy, what's the harm in that?"

"Harm?" Andy's angry voice shouted. "You make it sound like a joke,

Mrs. Maven."

"I don't see this as a joke and I'm sorry if I made it sound that way."

"So you'll stop?"

"Stop? Stop what? Stop talking to you? Stop visiting with Mr.

Rubenstein? What am I doing that is so awful?"

"Well, you're obviously doing something that's get-ting somebody upset enough to go to the trouble of threatening to kill you."

"Oh. That! But you did say you believed it was just to frighten me off, right?

"Yes. I did say that, but we don't know who we're dealing with here. If it's some kind of wacko, there's no telling what he or she can or will do."

"Are you saying that I shouldn't go to Mr. Rubenstein's apartment?" I couldn't believe I had to have permission to visit one of my neighbors.

"You're really making this a lot harder than it has to be." Andy said. Go visit Mr. Rubenstein. But for your information, and this is the only information I will give you from now on, we already have the tenant list and I have a team pouring over it as we speak."

"Oh." I said, surprised. So much for my optimistic belief that Mr. Rubenstein and I would single handedly be able to view the list and figure out who the murderer was. Just like that. Never mind that the police, who must have gotten the information from Nancy days ago, were still trying to come up with any solid leads from the list.

"You still there?" Andy asked.

"Yes. Just thinking of what you told me about having the list already."

"Takes the wind out of your sails, doesn't it?" Andy said softly.

"Yes, as a matter of fact, it does."

"Look. I don't mean to be disrespectful or give you a hard time. But for your own sake, for your family's sake, and for my peace of mind, please stay out of our investigation. Okay?"

I felt embarrassed at his rebuke, disappointed and a little contrite. But not enough to give up. There was still plenty of fight left in me.

"Andy?"

"Yes."

"I have one more question, or rather an observation."

"Go on."

I wondered at this point, if anything I told Andy would be considered relevant or even taken seriously. I probably should have hung up, but my tenacious nature kept pushing me forward, so I plowed right in. I filled

Andy in on my visit to Helen Brunner's apartment on Saturday and then again that afternoon at the library. I described how different she seemed on Saturday, both in appearance and in attitude and then today, when she had seemed abrupt and almost rude at my attempt to be friendly.

"And why is any of this relevant?"

"Because I think she might be holding back more information than she first shared."

Silence.

"Andy?"

"I'm here. What you're telling me is certainly interesting, but I'm not convinced it's a sign of any criminal intent."

"Well maybe not, but doesn't it strike you as a little strange?"

"Strange? Yes. I'll agree to strange, but strange is not a criminal offense either. Still…."

"What?"

"Uh, nothing. I just had a thought about what you said earlier. You might actually be onto something, but I have to check it out."

"Really? What?" Could I really have given Andy a clue to work with?

"Something John Brunner said during the interrogation. I was just thinking out loud. Mrs. Maven?"

"Yes Andy?"

"You will be careful, won't you?" He sounded distracted, but his tone had softened considerably.

"Of course," I said as we both said goodbye and hung up. I would have liked to have questioned Andy about what it was I said that had him thinking I might actually be on to something, but I knew he wouldn't tell me.

I took a deep breath. Now all I had to do was come clean with Milt, bring him up to date on all activities since he left this morning and hope that if the killer didn't succeed in his attempt to kill me, Milt wouldn't try to do it for him!

CHAPTER TWENTY-ONE

"So you went to see Mr. Rubenstein today?" The sound of Milt's voice startled me.

"I didn't hear you come in? How long have you been here?" I asked, although the more important question was, how much did he hear?

"I thought you promised you wouldn't continue investigating." Milt dropped his briefcase on the kitchen table.

"I stopped by to see how Mr. Rubenstein was doing because he's a lonely old man who just lost his son. What is so wrong about visiting him?"

"Nothing, if that was the only reason. However, from what you told Andy, it seems like it was more than just a friendly visit."

"I asked a few questions as part of our general conversation. Believe it or not Milt, he was as interested in talking about this as I was."

"That I find hard to believe. Especially from a man who hardly ever opens his mouth." Milt was leaning against the sink, arms folded across his chest.

"You saw how he was after the funeral, how he opened up. He seemed very comfortable with my visit. We had tea and talked."

"And what's this about a visit to the library? Was it really to check out Harry Potter books or was Helen Brunner your real incentive?"

"I wanted the Harry Potter books, Milt. Now enough of this inquisition before it gets out of hand again."

"*Oy*, Sadie. What am I'm supposed to say? Between the car and that threatening call, I'm worried sick about you. This whole morning I kept thinking of you, wondering where you were going, what you were doing and if you were all right."

"I'm sorry you feel that way. Andy said he thought whoever is behind the car and the call is just trying to scare me off and doesn't exactly want to kill me."

"And that's supposed to make be feel better? Don't you see, whoever is doing this isn't going to stop at just trying to scare you off. This whole thing could escalate."

"Oh for goodness sakes, Milt, enough already. It's not like I'm running around with a gun or trailing people into dark corners. The call has successfully managed to frighten me. Okay? I'm scared. I will be careful, but I am certainly not going to lock myself in the apartment for the rest of the time it takes for the police to find Sol's killer."

Without saying another word, Milt turned and walked out of the room.

It was going to be a long afternoon. I emptied the dishwasher, made a second attempt to start the Harry Potter book and found that I couldn't concentrate on anything.

At some point I checked my refrigerator with the intention of preparing dinner. Fortunately I had last night's leftovers so I didn't have to give that much thought.

I took the food out of the Styrofoam containers, placed it in a bowl, and heated it in the microwave. I prepared a salad of salvageable greens, tomatoes and peppers, and warmed up the bread we had taken home from the restaurant. I even found an assortment of fruit which, once the over ripe parts were discarded, made a fairly presentable fruit salad. All things considered, it wasn't a bad dinner, other than the fact that neither of us said much.

After cleaning up the kitchen, I grabbed my keys and a sweater. I walked over to Milt, who was working on the doll house which, I had to admit, was actually taking shape nicely.

"You're doing a great job. Julie's going to love this."

"Thanks." Milt continued sanding one of the pieces of wood.

"Okay. Well, I'm going down to see Mr. Rubenstein. I won't be long."

"Again?' Milt stopped sanding and looked at me. "You were there this afternoon." Apparently Milt hadn't heard that part of my conversation with Andy.

I nodded. "I told Mr. Rubenstein that I'd come back in the evening." I reached over and gave Milt a kiss on his forehead. "I'm sorry you're so upset by all this. I love you."

"I know. Me too." He reached for my hand. "Just be careful, okay?"

I closed the door softly behind me and started for the stairs. I walked down slowly, worrying about Milt and how sad he looked when I left. I was feeling guilty again and sad too at what this whole murder thing had done to so many lives. But I wasn't about to give up, to turn back and simply return to our apartment and sit and watch television or read a book. Not while there were so many unanswered questions. I simply would not rest until all the pieces were lined up neatly in a row and there was closure for everyone.

I reached the ground floor, mindful of the area that held Sol's body less than a week ago. As I approached Mr. Rubenstein's apartment, a heavyset woman passed me in the lobby. We nodded politely at each other and continued in our opposite directions. I knocked on Mr. Rubenstein's door and was surprised when he answered so quickly.

"Were you waiting at the door for me?" I asked, half in jest.

"No." Mr. Rubenstein answered, holding the door open for me to enter. "Nancy just left. You probably passed her in the hall."

"I believe I did, only I didn't realize who she was. She brought you the printout of the apartment rentals and vacancies?"

"Yes. Here, sit down. Take a look, it's very interesting."

After having gotten Mr. Rubenstein all fired up about the tenant list and the possibility of finding the killer from among all the names, I didn't have the heart to tell him that the police already had this information and so far, no leads.

Playing along, I spread out the comprehensive printout. Maybe I'd get lucky and find something the police missed. Unlikely, but still a possibility.

Of the thirty-two apartments on the four upper floors, eight were vacant, one was rented but not occupied yet, and another one was not currently occupied because the tenants were away in Europe for several months.

"That reduces the number of apartments to twenty-two." I said, mentally scrolling down the list. "That's approximately forty tenants, assuming a few single occupancies. We know the Paceys weren't in that night, and I know it wasn't you, Milt or I, or Mrs. Pinsky for that matter, so that brings it to thirty-four."

"There are too many people to account for." Mr. Rubenstein said, sounding disappointed. "We couldn't possibly question or track down each and every one of those tenants."

I nodded. If the police were still working on this, how in the world had I ever thought we would be more successful.

"So what do we do now?" Mr. Rubenstein asked.

"I think the best thing to do is let the police figure it out." I could see the disappointment on Mr. Rubenstein's face. I felt sorry for giving him false hope.

"It's okay," I tried to make it sound optimistic. "We gave it our best shot. I'm sure the police will be able to do something with this."

I hugged him gently, told him I'd stop by later in the week and let myself out.

I returned to the apartment. Milt was still working on the dollhouse, making slow, but steady progress. We exchanged small talk. I admired his work again, he asked about Mr. Rubenstein. We verbally danced around each other, avoiding any explosive issues that would be triggered with the wrong word or nuance.

As I watched Milt work, I thought how easy it would have been to have promised him that I had, once and for all, stopped my personal involvement in the case. I'm sure he would have been relieved and very pleased. But I couldn't make that promise.

I took a deep breath. I am not giving up, I repeated to myself. I'm tenacious. I'm determined and I'm stubborn. Looking back now, I should have added, and foolish!

CHAPTER TWENTY-TWO

Tuesday morning was another sunny, spring-like day. Unfortunately it did little to improve either my mood or my lethargy.

I woke up at six o'clock feeling groggy. I had had trouble falling asleep at first and then when I did, I had weird dreams again. This time I dreamt of being chased, getting lost, and misplacing my earrings. I tried to stay in bed a while longer, but it was no use.

Milt was still asleep, snoring softly as he lay on his back with his mouth open. I finally dragged myself out of bed as quietly as I could and went into the kitchen. I made coffee and poured myself a glass of orange juice.

Milt woke up soon after. He walked into the kitchen, still in his pajamas and slippers.

"I smell coffee," he said, grabbing a cup from the cupboard. "Is it ready?"

"Yes, help yourself." I said, stifling a yawn.

"You didn't have a very good night, did you?" He asked, pouring himself a cup.

"Nope. Sorry if I disturbed you with my tossing and turning."

"You didn't. I woke up myself a few times and saw how restless you were. You must be tired."

"I am, but I'm going out soon to pick up food and other stuff. The fresh air will wake me up."

Our conversation continued in this neutral patter as we finished breakfast. We were in one of those out-of-sync moments, which neither of us liked, but didn't know quite how to get out of.

Milt got dressed, then went into the other room to work on his project. I made a few phone calls for a fundraising committee I was on and by ten, I showered and dressed for my outing.

I peeked in on Milt to tell him I was leaving.

"Sadie," Milt said, putting his tools on the bench and turning to me. "I'm sorry we can't seem to get back on the same wave length. I don't like it when we're off like this. I know you're angry at me for not being more understanding. But can we move on? Can we be friends again? I miss you."

Truth was I missed Milt too. I missed our closeness and our ability to tell each other our thoughts, opinions, dreams, and fears, without the other one becoming angry or judgmental. These past few days had been an emotional see-saw. Milt had been right about not being supportive. That had made me angry and that's what I couldn't let go of now.

He stood waiting for my response, reaching out to me, while I stood passive. Oh, for goodness sake, I scolded myself. Let it go.

I turned to Milt. "Me too." I said, moving closer to him. He put his arms around me and kissed me.

"Do you want me to go to with you?" He asked, still holding me in his arms. "I could help you with the packages."

"No. I'll be fine. I'll take the grocery cart with me. It holds a lot. Besides, I know you want to finish the doll house. But thanks for asking." I smiled.

Milt didn't push. I went to the kitchen, picked up my purse, my keys, my grocery list and my grocery cart. I was almost out the door when Milt called from the other room.

"Don't forget to pick up some cake for tonight. It's bridge night."

"What? I stopped at the door, puzzled. Aren't we going to Mindy and Jack's house?"

"No." Milt answered, walking into the hallway. "I'm sorry, I forgot to tell you. Mindy called last night after you had gone to bed. She said Jack came down with the flu so they wouldn't be able to host it. Since we're next on the rotation list anyway, I said it would okay to have it here. It is okay, isn't it?"

"Sure, of course." I would have liked a little more notice, but at least Milt remembered to tell me before I left for the store instead of after I returned.

Thank goodness hosting bridge night only involved dessert. That made it easy. I would stop by the bakery on the way home and pick up a crumb cake and some cookies.

I was looking forward to the walk, counting on my errands to take my mind off the events of the past few days. I inhaled deeply, hoping to clear my head.

I stopped at the grocery store, went next door to the bakery and then the bank. Walking home, I passed a sports store specializing in athletic shoes and decided to pick up a new pair of cross trainers.

Balancing my purse, my new purchase and the Benton's Bakery box with one hand, and pulling the shopping cart with my other hand, I made my way out the door of the shoe store. As I headed home, I noticed Helen Brunner across the street, walking quickly in the opposite direction.

It was almost noon by then. I knew she worked from twelve to four on Tuesdays and Thursdays. She should have been heading in the other direction, towards the library, but she wasn't. Hmmm, maybe her hours had changed, or maybe she took the day off. Well, it certainly wasn't important, nor was it any of my business. Still, she sure seemed in a hurry.

I continued to think about Helen as I walked the short distance to the apartment building. Where could she have been going? She was heading towards the train station. Maybe she was off to visit her husband. Maybe I just needed to stop with all my obsessing.

It was close to 12:30 when I returned. Milt was at the kitchen table reading the newspaper.

We took tentative steps towards polite conversation as we ate a light lunch. I didn't tell Milt about seeing Helen Brunner, or any related questions and thoughts I had had about her. Although things appeared to have improved between us, I felt we were still working our way past the emotionally charged atmosphere of the past week.

After lunch, Milt went into the living room. He said he had hit a plateau in his enthusiasm to finish the doll house and decided to take a break. I went next door to visit with Mrs. Pinsky. I hadn't seen her since Sunday and was anxious to see how she was doing. I was also curious to know if she and Mr. Rubenstein had had any more contact.

"Hello." She greeted me with a big smile.

"How are you feeling?" I asked.

"I feel fine. And why not? I got a good clean bill of health from that young doctor who checked me out Friday."

"Good. I'm glad to hear that." I said. Suddenly I got a whiff of something strange coming from Mrs. Pinsky's kitchen.

"What's that smell?"

"Oh," she responded sheepishly. "My daughter made delicious butter cookies while I was with her. They melted in my mouth so I asked her for the recipe. I was anxious to make it first thing this morning. I wanted to bring it to Mr. Rubenstein. When I got half way through adding the ingredients, I realized I didn't have butter or even margarine, so I substituted a little chicken fat I had left over. It was a big mistake! I should have known better."

"Oh, you could've asked me." I suppressed a laugh. "I went food shopping this morning. I would have picked up whatever you needed."

"It doesn't matter. I have other cookies in the freezer. I'll bring that to him later. So, sit down and tell me, what's going on? Any new developments in the police investigation since I saw you last?"

"No, not really." I answered, avoiding any mention of the threatening phone call.

"Nothing? How could there be nothing new?" she asked. "You mean you haven't spoken to anyone? Not your detective friend, not Mrs. Brunner, no one else in the building? How could that be?"

"Yes, of course I've spoken to them, but…." I was reluctant to go on, afraid of getting pulled back into the excitement of discussing the details.

"But what?" She looked at me, waiting for an answer, or at least more details.

"Well, it's complicated," I said, adding that I was no longer convinced that John was in fact the killer.

I recounted the favorable comments I had heard regarding John Brunner. "Carol and Bill each offered pretty positive points of view regarding John. Both said, in so many words, that they couldn't picture him being a murderer."

"Well for goodness sakes, Mrs. Maven, what do they think, that John Brunner's too nice to have killed anyone? I bet the mother of Son of Sam also thought her son was too nice to be a murderer."

Sometimes, Mrs. Pinsky's comments require no response. This was one of those times.

"Well, to be fair, Mrs. Pinsky, their comments did get me thinking about John and whether or not he was guilty. I mean, doesn't it seem strange to you that a wife suspects her husband almost immediately after a murder has occurred, and then quickly shares that suspicion with someone else, encouraging that individual to inform the police?"

"No, not really," the ever pragmatic Mrs. Pinsky replied. "Not if she has good reason to suspect him. There was a movie I saw, a while ago, where the wife thinks her husband's guilty and she tells someone who then has the husband killed." Mrs. Pinsky stared blankly for a moment. "Or, something like that. Whatever, it probably happens more often then you think."

"Maybe in the movies," I said, "but in this case, I can't help thinking that there has to be more reasons to suspect John. Just because he was angry during the meeting and stormed out soon after, doesn't mean he's a killer. And the fact that he didn't go where his wife thought he was going, well, how valid is that? Apparently he never said he was going there in the first place. Helen just assumed that was where he was going. Maybe he was meeting a friend, or took in a movie."

"But didn't you tell me that the police must have thought he was guilty or they wouldn't have arrested him?" Mrs. Pinsky persisted.

"Yes, but the papers mentioned that the police are now questioning whether John is the one who killed Sol after all, although Andy's department refuses to officially comment on that."

"Really? Well I don't see how they can be so wishy washy about something like this. Either he did it or he didn't," Mrs. Pinsky said in a petulant tone.

I ignored her comment. Suddenly, feeling tired and depressed, I put my head in my hands. "Oh, Mrs. Pinsky, I don't know what to do. My kids aren't happy that I became so personally involved, Milt's upset, Andy's becoming more and more concerned and even Helen Brunner seems very strange lately.

"But you can't just give up. This isn't like you."

"I know. But it's time for me to back off. Let it go and just let the police handle it. At least I won't have my whole family jumping down my throat and making jokes about my being a P.I."

"P.I.?"

"Yes. P.I. and whatever combination of words my family finds appropriate at the moment. Private investigator, personally involved, persistently insistent, particularly intrusive. You name it."

Mrs. Pinsky laughed. "I've known you a long time, Mrs. Maven, but I've never heard that before. How long has that been going on?"

"Oh, I'd say for some time now, ever since I started finding missing keys, misplaced items, whatever." I took a deep breath and sighed. "Mrs. Pinsky, I don't snoop? Do I? I mean, I'm not pushy or nosey. Am I?"

"No. Come on, cheer up. Look at all the good you've done for people since Sol's death."

"Oh please. What have I possibly done that could even remotely be classified as good?"

"Well, for one thing, you helped Sol's father with the funeral arrangements. You've helped the police by giving them information, you've been very good to Helen Brunner, and, you brought Morris and me together."

"Morris and you? I'd almost forgotten. How is that coming along?"

"Coming along? I don't know what you mean by coming along, but we do see each other from time to time. I bring him food, he returns the plates in the morning. We talk, we visit. He's very nice company for me. In fact, I was there last evening. He invited me to have tea and watch television with him."

"Did you?" I asked.

"Yes, of course. We had a lovely time."

"Oh, you must have arrived right after I left his apartment."

"That's what Morris told me when I got there. He said he had had a busy evening beginning with his son's assistant stopping by, your visit and then my visit. I think he enjoys the attention and activity."

"I'm sure he does. He's been lonely for such a long time."

"He's invited me over again this evening.

"Did he tell you about our little theory?"

"The one about the number of rented or vacant apartments on the upper floors? Yes and it's not a bad idea, although I don't know how you'd be able to use it to figure out who the killer is."

"Neither do I. I was going to give that information to Andy but they already have the lists. I don't think it's all that helpful or relevant, but maybe the police will be able to find something useful in it."

"So, you're really off the case?"

"Yes I am." I said with conviction, although a part of me remained unconvinced.

"I see." She gave me a shy smile, as though she had been reading my thoughts.

"Well. Anyway. I'm happy to hear that you and Morris Rubenstein are, you know, friends. It's good to have company. He's a good man. I like him."

"I do too." Mrs. Pinsky said. "It's strange how things happen. But I guess everything happens for a reason."

"Yes that's true. Meanwhile, I think it's wonderful and I'm glad it's working out for the both of you."

I stood up to leave. "Oh, I almost forgot to tell you. They found the Dudley boys. In Utah of all places."

"Utah? What were they doing there?" She asked.

"Apparently responding to a job opportunity."

"Are they okay?

"Oh, they're fine. In fact they didn't even know they were missing until someone read about them in the newspaper and pointed it out to them. They went to the police department in Utah to straighten it all out."

"So they're not suspects in Sol's murder?" Mrs. Pinsky asked.

"No. I guess they never were. The police just wanted to talk to them since they had been at the meeting. When they didn't show up anywhere, the police became concerned that something might have happened to them.

"Well I'm glad they're all right. I don't exactly like them, but I wouldn't want to see any one else get hurt."

"I agree," I said, walking towards the door.

"So what happens now?" she asked.

"Now? Now I'll return to my apartment. Try to keep the peace with Milt and think about dinner. We have our bridge group coming tonight. That should help take my mind off the investigation."

"Good luck," she said as she closed the door.

CHAPTER TWENTY-THREE

When I returned to the apartment, I found a note from Milt telling me that he had an errand to run and would be back around four. I checked the answering machine and found a message from Frannie, asking me to call her back, ASAP. Very concerned when there's an ASAP attached to a message from my children, I called back immediately.

"Hi." I said. "What happened? Are the kids okay?"

"The kids?" She sounded surprised. "Of course they're okay. Why?"

"Because your message said to call back ASAP. I was worried that something happened to one of you."

"No. Mother. I was calling because of you."

"Me? What are you talking about?"

"I spoke to Dad this morning. You had just left to do your shopping. He filled me in on everything, the car almost running over you and your little call last night."

"Oh that. Everything's okay. I'm fine. Your father tends to exaggerate sometimes, Frannie. He shouldn't have upset you by telling you.

"Of course he should have Mother. In fact, you should have called me right away. If any of this had happened to me, you'd want to know about that, wouldn't you?"

"Well, yes, of course. But that's different." I wondered how I was going to get myself off the hook on this one.

"No, it's not different. Are you kidding? A car almost runs you down, then you get a threatening call. This is very serious. You shouldn't keep something like this from Paul or me."

"Okay, okay. Frannie, you're right, I should have called but I didn't want you to become upset, as you obviously are. The whole thing is some sick plan to scare me away from asking questions about Sol's murder."

"Mother, how can you be so blasé about this? Have you called the police?"

"Yes, as a matter of fact, I have."

"And…?"

"And what? The police agree that the guy is probably just trying to scare me, not kill me, Frannie. I know that sounds bad, but let's not make it worse than it is."

"How can you say that? I'm frightened to death about this and you're telling me it's nothing."

"No, I'm not saying it's nothing, I'm just saying that it's under control. The police know about the call and they're looking into it. And, just to reassure you once and for all, as it happens I've stopped asking questions and trying to be personally involved in this whole thing. See, the guy succeeded in scaring me off the case, so now you can stop worrying."

Silence.

"Really?" Frannie replied, sounding slightly relieved.

"Yes. Really. I'm not pursuing this any more. Whatever happens or whatever information I hear, I'll pass it on directly to Andy, the detective I told you about who's working the case."

"Good. If you really mean that, then I can relax a little. I'm sorry I was so upset before, but I became completely unglued after Dad told me what had happened."

"I know and I don't blame you, although I do blame your father for scaring you like that. And I'm going to let him know how I feel, too."

"Mom, don't go after Dad. He's worried sick over this. He doesn't have anyone else to vent to, so when I called he just opened up. I'm sure I wasn't much help to him once he told me and I probably made him feel worse than he made me feel. Don't be too hard on him."

"Fine, I'll go easy on him, although that's probably why he conveniently forgot to tell me about your call. He knew I'd be upset with him for telling you."

With the drama of the car and threatening call no longer the focus of the conversation, we moved on to a recap of Julie's gymnastic class that morning and Dan's class excursion to a neighborhood doughnut shop.

"Can you imagine, all these little six-year-olds watching the machines mass produce those fabulous doughnuts? Then they got to have samples. God, I'm glad I wasn't one of the parent chaperones on this trip. Doughnuts hot from the oven, I'd never be able to stop at one."

"I know exactly what you mean," I laughed, relieved that our conversation was winding down on a happy note. We chatted a few more minutes before hanging up.

Milt walked in a little before four. I was tempted to bring up Frannie's frantic call but decided not to press the issue. We were on such tenuous footing, I couldn't bring myself to cause anymore chaos.

I did tell him about my visit with Mrs. Pinsky and the budding relationship between her and Mr. Rubenstein. It felt good to be able to share tidbits like this without fear of upsetting either of us.

"Good for her," he chuckled. "She's quite a spunky lady, maybe she's too much for poor old Mr. Rubenstein."

"Oh, I don't know. I think they'd make an adorable couple."

"Uh, oh. Now you're meddling in their social lives?"

"No, I'm not meddling. They're doing that all on their own." I bristled at Milt's choice of words.

Maybe I was still a little sensitive, however meddling, in my opinion, sounded a little too much like snooping and as far Mrs. Pinsky and Mr. Rubenstein's social lives were concerned, I was nowhere near that stage ...yet!

CHAPTER TWENTY-FOUR

I took a deep breath and let my moment of "bristling" pass. I reassured myself that Milt's use of the word, meddle, was really meant as a joke this time, with no hidden element of truth.

After dinner, we pushed the coffee table away from the couch and over to the side wall. We set up the bridge tables and chairs in the middle of the room. In the kitchen, Milt prepared coffee, while I took out the cups, saucers and dessert plates. I placed them along side the linen napkins and silverware I had already set out on the kitchen table. Then I took the crumb cake and cookies from the bakery box and arranged them on a large square shaped serving platter.

Feeling satisfied with the appearance of the kitchen table and all its abundance, I went into the bedroom to change into black wool pants and a red sweater set. I ran a comb through my hair in a futile attempt to fluff it into some semblance of style and order. It was naturally curly and seldom did what I wanted it to do.

As I walked out of the bedroom, I remembered the crystal earrings Amanda made for me. Milt had not fixed the earring yet, but I thought it would be safe to wear it since I was going to be home all evening.

I figured if the earring fell out again it would fall somewhere in the house and hopefully be easily found.

I put the earrings on, pleased that I had remembered. Amanda would be thrilled when I told her I had worn them this evening for our friends to see.

The doorbell rang and we welcomed our guests. They were all fun people to be with and we always looked forward to our monthly bridge games with them. Since dessert first was an unspoken rule of bridge, at least with our group, we headed straight for the kitchen. As Milt often quipped, life's too short, eat dessert first. So we did.

Standing around the kitchen table making small talk, Sandy, one of our bridge group regulars, suddenly noticed my earrings.

"Wow! What great earrings. They're so unusual. Where'd you find them? I'd love to have a pair like that. They'd go great with a new dress I just bought. The crystals have the same multicolored tones as the dress."

"Amanda made them for me," I answered proudly.

"Amanda made them for you? I can't believe it." She took a closer look. "They look professional."

"I know. I thought the same thing. Apparently she'd been at a birthday party where an artist demonstrated the art of jewelry making. My daughter-in-law made Amanda promise to create a similar pair for her."

"Well, tell her if she wants to earn extra money, I'll pay her to make a pair for me too." Sandy said.

"Actually, I wouldn't mind earrings like that either," Brenda, a fairly new addition to the group said as she came closer to inspect them. "She did a great job. I've seen crystal earrings at art fairs that don't come close to these. Your granddaughter has talent and you can tell her I said so."

"You bet I will. Thanks, she'll be very pleased." I touched my right ear lightly, making sure the earring was still securely in place.

We continued to stand around the table for a while, eating and talking.

Neither Milt nor I brought up the topic of Sol Rubenstein's murder and we were pleased to see that it wasn't a number one topic of interest for our company either.

Once the refreshments were out of the way, we headed to the living room. We were just sitting down to begin playing when the phone rang.

I could have let the answering machine pick up, but I thought it might be one of my kids still concerned about me, so I rushed to the kitchen to pick up. We have a portable phone in the bedroom, but I'd forgotten to take it with me before the guests had arrived. At this point, it was easier to grab the kitchen phone than to go into the bedroom for the other one.

"Hello." I said.

"Mrs. Maven? It's Helen Brunner. I'm so sorry to bother you, but something terrible has happened. I need your help." She sounded tense and slightly out of breath.

"My goodness, are you all right?"

"No. I'm very upset. I just found some papers in my bedroom. I think they belong to John. I don't know for sure, but I might have made a terrible mistake about John being the one who killed Sol Rubenstein.

You were right with your comments the other day. Remember when you said that you and Mr. Rubenstein didn't see John as the murderer. I didn't take it seriously at the time, but now, with these papers, I think you might be right. Could you come up to my apartment and take a look at them? I'm so confused and frightened. Maybe you'll be able to tell me what you think I should do."

"Shouldn't you call the police?"

"No. Not yet. I mean, it might not be anything, then I'd feel foolish. But if I'm right, if you think I'm right, then of course I'll call right away. Mrs. Maven, I might have been a little abrupt when I saw you at the library and I apologize. I don't want you to be angry at me. I know calling you now is an imposition, but I really do need your help. I trust you. It wouldn't take very long. Please. I don't know who else I could turn to."

I hesitated. She sounded so vulnerable. I didn't want to do this, not now, not with Milt here and our guests. And I was trying so hard to get past all this stuff and not be involved anymore.

"Uh, couldn't it wait until tomorrow?"

"I suppose it could," she sighed. "It's just that if I was wrong about John, I wouldn't want him staying in jail any longer than necessary. But, you're right." she sounded subdued. "I guess it could wait. One more night in the jail won't kill him."

Guilt. Just what I needed. I was torn. I didn't want to go, but on the other hand, I'll admit I was curious. Besides, what was the harm in going up? I'd check it out and be back within five minutes, ten at the most.

"Okay," I finally agreed. "I'll be right up."

It's a small apartment, so of course everyone heard my end of the conversation. When I returned to the living room, the look on Milt's face was not a happy one.

"I have to leave for just five minutes," I told Milt and the others, trying to keep my voice light. "One of my neighbors is having a tough time and needs to show me something, something important." I looked around the table at blank stares. No one was buying this, so I decided to come clean.

"Okay. It's Helen Brunner. She thinks she's found something in the apartment that could prove her husband's innocence, but she's not sure. She trusts my judgment and wants me to take a look. That's it. No big deal. Why don't you visit, have some more coffee and dessert. I promise I'll be right back in no time. You won't even notice I'm gone." Ha! Ha!

"Oh. So it's true," Amy said, drawing out each word. She and her husband Ted, were our substitute players and while they were good at cards, Amy had a reputation of being somewhat of a royal pot stirrer, thrilled with the opportunity to stir things up whenever and wherever she could.

"My, oh, my, you're still doing your sleuthing," she continued with a well tuned flair for the dramatic. "I ran into your neighbor, Mrs. Pinsky, last week and she told me all about it. She said you were taking charge of the investigation. At least I think that was how she put it."

"It's more like plain old fashioned persistent interfering, if you ask me," Milt muttered not quite under his breath.

"Milt…"

"Well, I think it's very exciting having a murder suspect right in your own back yard, and then having the suspect's wife as a personal friend." Ted offered. "There could be a story in this for you, you know, a book or a made for television movie."

"Uh, well, I'm not so sure of that Ted, but I'll keep it in mind. I better get going now so I can come right back." I hurried out, hoping to make quick work of this. I heard the phone ringing again as the door closed behind me.

I took the stairs up to the sixth floor, thinking about the timing of her call. Too bad it couldn't have been in the morning. I wouldn't have had to contend with everyone's opinions and judgments.

I walked to her apartment, took a deep breath and knocked. Helen Brunner opened immediately. She was wearing jeans and a pink turtleneck that made her look very young and vulnerable. What a chameleon, I thought to myself.

"Thank you for coming up so quickly." She spoke quickly and looked slightly pale. I didn't give it much more thought, assuming it might have had to do with high anxiety over whatever it was that she had found.

"I don't know what I'd do without you. You're the only one I felt I could call." She opened the door wide, allowing me to pass ahead of her.

"The papers are in the living room, on the table straight ahead," she continued talking, as I walked forward.

The lighting was soft. The apartment was quiet, almost eerie in its silence. Since Sol's murder I've gone through a myriad of emotions, including shock, disbelief, sadness, anger, confusion and even outrage. Now, for the first time since last Wednesday, I felt goose bumps on my arms and an overwhelming sense of fear.

Approaching the table, where several papers were haphazardly spread out, I suddenly had a sense of someone approaching from the shadows at my side. As I turned, I caught a glimpse of an object rapidly coming towards me. I instinctively raised my arms to ward if off, but I wasn't fast enough. Something hard and solid caught me on the side of my head. I felt my head explode with excruciating pain.

As I went down, I heard a man's voice shouting for tape at the same time I saw small flashing lights. My brain must have been seriously damaged at that point because I could have sworn I'd seen those lights before. In fact, I was certain they had been on a pair of loafers in the strangest combination of green and purple I'd ever seen.

CHAPTER TWENTY-FIVE

W hen I opened my eyes, I was lying face down on a thin carpet. My hands were tied behind my back and tape held my mouth tightly shut. Movement was impossible. In addition to my awkward position on the floor, my head hurt with what I can only describe as the mother of all headaches.

I know I slipped in and out of consciousness, because I had no concept of time. At some point I heard muffled sounds coming from another room. It was difficult to concentrate on the words and my headache wasn't helping.

"Open the door carefully and look outside," someone with a deep voice was saying. "If it's clear, I'll untie her, carry her out to the stairs and then you pull off the gag before I push her over."

I heard laughter.

"They'll find her like they found Sol. The police won't have a clue."

They were talking about me. Me! Oh God! They were going to kill me. It was surreal. This couldn't be happening. It had to be another nightmare. My mind was playing tricks on me. Yes, of course, that's what this was. But even as I thought this and wished with all my heart for that to be true, I knew it wasn't.

My heart was racing. With each breath I took in dust and carpet fibers. I sneezed and a streak of pain went through me like an electric current. This was definitely not a dream. This was for real and there were people in the next room who were going to kill me.

I couldn't die. Not here. Not like this. I struggled against my restraints and felt the stabbing pain in my head. I tried to breathe, to think, to hope. I thought of Milt being alone, agonizing over my death. I thought of my children and grandchildren and all the celebrations and life cycle events that would take place without me. I couldn't bear it. My nose was running and I was crying.

I had to get out of here, but how? I wasn't even sure I knew where here was. The last thing I remember was being in Helen Brunner's apartment. That could have been hours ago. Maybe they moved me. Oh God! What in heavens name am I going to do?

I tried really hard to concentrate.

Suddenly I heard banging on a door. Then shouting. I strained to hear the muffled sounds.

"Police. Open the door."

I heard footsteps, then a woman's voice. "Quick, go into the bedroom and stay with her. Here, take the bat and hit her again if she makes any sounds. I'll take care of the cops."

That was Helen Brunner's voice. Even in my haze I recognized her distinctive whiney voice. What was going on here?

Then it hit me, no pun intended. I had an epiphany. She was the killer all along. She was in on it with someone...of course....the man with the strange shoes.

My God! Sol's bodyguard. The tall one. He was the one who came at me with the bat. Somehow he must have returned after the tenant meeting without being seen and managed to get Sol up to the apartment. They hit Sol with the bat then they dragged his semi unconscious body to the stairs, where they pushed him over the hand rail to his death. What an idiot I was to be taken in so easily by Helen Brunner.

The sound of a door being opened nearby interrupted my scrambled thoughts. I heard footsteps approaching, heavy breathing, then a menacing voice close to my face.

"One sound out of you and you get a reunion with the bat. Understand?"

I nodded, bringing forth more torrents of pain.

More banging. Another muffled sound. Helen's voice: "I'm coming."

The sound of a door being opened and then several footsteps moving about in the next room.

"Where is she? We know she's here. Don't make this worse for yourself than it already is."

Andy? Was I really hearing Andy's voice?

"I don't know what you're talking about." Helen Brunner whined. "There's no one here but me." She was shouting now, feigning outrage and defiance. "Why can't you leave me alone? You took my husband, you destroyed my marriage, now you're trying to destroy me."

She was ranting, but why and to whom? Why was Andy here? What was going on?

I strained to hear more.

"You called Mrs. Maven. We know she's here." I was pretty certain that was Andy's voice. How did he know or even manage to get here so fast?

"You asked her to come up. Where is she?"

Milt? That was Milt's voice. Was Milt here too? He must have followed me when I left the apartment.

"No. That's a lie." Helen whined.

I squirmed as I tried to make noise, wanting somehow to let Milt know that I was here. I wanted him to forgive me for causing him such pain. Poor man, he must be beside himself with fear for my life.

"Shut up, bitch," my attacker hissed in my ear. "One more sound and you're dead. Right here, right now."

"Calm down, Mr. Maven. Let us handle this." That was definitely Andy's voice.

Oh Milt. I am so sorry. What did I do? What did I do to us?

There were more voices. Milt was shouting.

"Andy, look. It's her earring. She was wearing it this evening when she left the apartment. She has to be here. It hasn't been that long. She's here, I know she's here."

My earring? It must have fallen out when I was hit and fell to the ground.

I heard footsteps, a door opening and suddenly, bright lights.

"Drop it!" It was Andy's voice.

A hard object fell across my leg.

Hands were removing the tape. I felt Milt's arms around me as he gently lifted me in his arms.

"Milt.... I'm so sorry....." I moved my head towards him to speak, bringing still another wave of pain and nausea.

"It's okay, sweetheart. You're okay, that's all that matters. I love you so much."

I heard his voice catch and felt a tear as he kissed me tenderly on my cheek. I felt warmed and comforted by Milt's voice. I wanted to say more, to tell Milt how much I loved him, but the words wouldn't come. I felt the tears running down my face as I slipped slowly, peacefully into a sea of darkness.

CHAPTER TWENTY-SIX

I woke up in a hospital room. A very pale looking Milt was hovering over the bed. Andy and his partner, Brian Masters, were pacing nearby.

"Oooooh." I was groggy and my head hurt like hell. "Where am I? What happened?"

Milt looked at Andy, who came over as soon as he saw I was awake.

"I think it's fair to say you had a tumble with the Devil and came out the winner," Andy said in a serious tone. "Of course it would have been better if you hadn't allowed yourself that opportunity. But thank goodness it all turned out okay. You were very lucky."

"You're in the hospital," Milt said as he held my hand. "You have a slight concussion, but the doctor says that will heal with time and rest. Considering that you were smacked with a baseball bat by a six-foot-two former high school football player, it could have been a lot worse."

"I don't understand." I closed my eyes, trying to grab bits and pieces of memory as they floated past.

"Oh!" I shuddered as I suddenly remembered. "Helen Brunner's apartment. I was hit on my head and fell down. I heard voices. Oh God. They were going to kill me, weren't they?"

Milt stroked my hand gently. "It's okay honey. You're safe. You're going to be fine."

"But I heard your voice Andy. How did you know where I was? And Milt, why were you there?" I looked at Andy, then Milt.

"As you were leaving our place the phone rang," Milt answered. "It was Andy. When I told him you had just left to go to Helen Brunner's apartment, he went crazy."

"Well, I didn't exactly go crazy, but I was disturbed to hear that your wife was headed to Mrs. Brunner's apartment," Andy explained.

Milt started to speak again but was interrupted by the nurse who came in to check my head wound, blood pressure, temperature and finally, to give me my blessed pain medication. When she left, Milt continued.

"Andy told me to go after you and stop you from going into her apartment. He said they were on their way. In fact, they were pulling up as we were speaking. He told me that they had reason to believe Helen might be the killer and that your life could be in danger. Hearing that, I ran after you without saying a word to our guests. Lord knows what they must have thought."

Seeing my dazed expression, Andy started from the beginning.

"Remember the theory you and Mr. Rubenstein had that whoever made the call to Sol that night had to be someone in the building?"

"Yes, but...." I was trying hard to put all the pieces together while my brain was still operating on slow mode.

"Well," Andy continued, "after you told me that you and Mr. Rubenstein were going to look over the list of tenants in the building, especially those on the upper floors, that rang a bell. I went back and checked my notes from John's interrogation. While he was ranting about not having done anything wrong, he told us to ask his wife about her interest in the tenants. He said she had been bugging him for weeks to figure out how many people lived in the building. He had asked her what difference it made, but she never answered. She had been acting weird lately, John admitted, so he decided to just let it go."

"But what was the connection between Helen's interest in the tenants and her possibly being the killer?" I was now totally confused.

"At first, there was no connection that we could see. But when I reread John's statement about Helen's preoccupation with the tenants in the building, I decided to dig a little deeper into her background."

"And you found out...what exactly?"

"It turns out she has a history of mental instability beginning in her teens. She has violent streaks and has to take meds to keep things under control."

"And John didn't know? Even after they were married?"

"No, he never knew. When they were first married she continued to take her pills but told John they were hormone pills."

"We discovered that she had stopped taking them a few months ago and the time frame corresponds to when John says she started acting strange," Andy's partner, Brian, added.

"I still don't understand why in the world Helen would want to kill Sol? I don't think they even knew each other." I was getting frustrated at my inability to follow Andy's line of reasoning.

"Helen's plan had originally been to kill her husband. She wanted a divorce but John refused."

"Refused?" I questioned. "Why would he refuse considering how bizarre her behavior had become?"

"According to John," Brian continued, "even though she was difficult to live with, he believed in the sanctity of marriage and wanted to try to make theirs work."

"But," Andy added, "Helen didn't want any part of that. She'd met this guy, Fred Porter, one of Sol's assistants, a few months earlier and they hit it off. They wanted to get married, but since John refused, Helen had to figure another way to get him out of the picture. When Fred told her that he had overheard Sol talking about the potential sale of the building, she came up with the plan to kill Sol and make it look like John did it."

"That's sick," I said.

"That's an understatement," Milt said.

"In her mental state," Andy explained, "killing her husband directly would have led the police to her. She decided that if Sol Rubenstein was murdered, she could steer suspicion to some of the neighbors, then eventually to her husband. He'd go to jail, she'd insist on a divorce and John would ultimately agree."

"And this Fred guy bought into all this?" I asked.

"Well, he isn't exactly the sharpest tool in the shed. Apparently it didn't take too much convincing on her part to get him to go along with it. She told him she had family money and they'd be able to go off to South America and live like royalty."

"She has family money?" I asked, yawning as the medication finally began to take effect.

Andy shook his head. "No, she made that up, but I guess he believed her. She almost succeeded. The sale upset a lot of people. The tenant meeting went badly. John was on record as having made a threat and then couldn't account for the time period when Sol was killed. She knew her husband well and had it all planned for the murder rap to fall on him."

"Sorry, but I still don't get why she kept asking John about the tenants. What did that have to do with her killing Sol?"

"Because once she knew about the pending sale of the building, she knew that somehow Sol would have to come and address the tenants. She didn't know exactly how or when, but she was certain that she would make it happen."

"And I played right into her hands."

"Unknowingly of course, but yes. She believed that by having a lot of angry people at the meeting they would get riled up, show their hostility by making threats and ultimately become potential suspects in the investigation. That would throw suspicion away from her and keep the police guessing for a while. The way she had it arranged, she was certain that all suspicion would eventually fall on John."

"But what if her plan didn't work?"

"Then she was prepared to make sure another one did, one way or another. That's what happened when she saw you last Friday. She was getting impatient that things weren't progressing as fast as she wanted them to, so she decided to go ahead with Plan B."

"Plan B?"

"Yes. Using you as a conduit to get us to look more closely at her husband as a suspect."

"Even though John didn't have anything to do with it?"

"That's right, but she was going to give you subtle suggestions that would make you think he might have been involved."

"And I was gullible enough to fall for it." Now besides confused and in pain, I felt dumb and used. Oh boy.

I let that information sink in for a few seconds before more loose ends popped up in my head. "But what about the meeting? We all heard John threaten Sol."

"That was all part of Helen's plan," Andy answered. "She pushed John to go to the meeting, convincing him that the two of them would be able to start a fuss and incite the neighbors. This way Sol would see how much of an impact the sale of the building had on the tenants and maybe change his mind."

"Why would she do that? Was she really interested in the building being sold?" I was trying hard to make sense of what Andy was telling me but nothing was making sense.

"No, not at all. She just wanted witnesses to see John angry and threatening. But then when John started yelling, she backed off. He asked her about it later and she said she had chickened out. He got mad, said that made him look bad, and that's when he stormed out of their apartment to avoid any more arguing."

"Ah! And that's when Helen called Sol, right?" I said, pleased that I was finally beginning to get it. "But Sol must have still been angry at John for all his rantings during the meeting, so how did Helen convince him to actually come up to her apartment?"

"Helen knew Sol wouldn't come if John was involved. So using Fred's cell phone, she called and apologized to Sol for her husband's behavior. Then she said that John was out and she had several of the neighbors in her apartment ready to talk to him. If he was willing to come up, she was certain they could work things out amicably and the sale would go though without any ugliness. She also insisted that it had to be right away in case John came back earlier than expected."

"Sol believed her?"

"Apparently. Helen admitted as much to us during our interrogation, bragging about how easy it had been to get him to come up."

"I had no idea she was such a good actress." I said. "That makes me feel a little better about being duped by her."

I yawned deeply, feeling the need to sleep but struggling to remain awake. I still had so many questions floating in my head.

"Helen had told me that John had a temper and verbally abused her. Was that a lie too?"

"Yes. Turns out Helen was actually the one with the temper. John told us Helen verbally abused him for years, but always in private. No one ever saw or heard anything directly from her. They only heard John's reactions, the yelling in the apartment, the disgusted tone he'd use in public. She knew how to push his buttons and get him mad. She was counting on the fact that since everyone believed he had a temper, that would keep the suspicion on him at a high level."

"I see," I exhaled, slowly closing my eyes.

"What a minute." I opened my eyes wide. "What day is it? I mean, the last thing I remember is going into Helen's apartment. That was our bridge night, uh, Tuesday evening, right?" I looked helplessly at Milt.

"Yes, it was," Milt responded softly.

I saw his eyes welling up and my heart almost broke, knowing I was the cause of his emotional state right now. I lifted my hand to touch his cheek. He cleared his throat before continuing.

"It's now Wednesday afternoon, sweetheart. You were drifting in and out of consciousness in the ambulance last night, and then at the hospital for a while until they were able to stabilize you. The doctors ran a bunch of tests before administering medication for the pain."

I took in what Milt said, nodding as I allowed my eyes to close again. Still not completely willing to let go, I asked sleepily what ultimately happened to Helen and Sol's assistant whose name I had already forgotten.

"Andy and Brian hauled them both off to the station where they were questioned most of the night," Milt answered, looking at Andy for confirmation.

"That's right," Andy said, filling in the rest. "We had them in different interrogation rooms and Fred pretty much gave it up immediately. He claimed that Helen was the mastermind behind it all, but agreed it was his cell phone that was used to lure Sol Rubenstein up to the apartment in the first place."

"He also used it when he made that threatening call to you," Brian added.

"Didn't you trace the calls Sol and I received once you knew about them?" My words were slurred at this point, but I couldn't stop with my questions.

"We did," Andy answered. "But it was a dead end. Fred had lifted it from a table in a crowded bar the night before Sol's murder. The original owner lives in Texas. He told us his cell phone had been stolen while he was on a business trip out here. He hadn't reported it because he was drunk and didn't want it to become a big deal with his wife or his boss."

"Wow! Lots of twists and turns to this," I mumbled.

Andy nodded. "Fred didn't know the cell phone would end up being used by Helen the following evening. He just took it because he could. Then Helen insisted he throw the phone away after he placed that threatening call to you."

"So he got lucky, didn't he?"

"I don't know about that," Andy rubbed his head. "I'd say his luck ran out when he met up with Helen Brunner."

"And this Fred," I asked, "he's the guy with the strange shoes, right?"

"That's right."

"But you told me he had an alibi."

"I know and I'm sorry about that. He had us all fooled. We knew he lived in an apartment building not far from here. When he returned home after seeing Sabrina to her condo, he made a point of making a lot

197

of noise opening his door. Dropped his keys, pounded on the door, slammed it shut, that sort of thing. It accomplished two things. One, it disturbed his neighbors who opened their doors to see what was going on and two, it established an alibi. It was a smart plan. I'm sure Helen set it all up for him."

"Then he snuck out?" In spite of everything that had happened, I actually felt a glimmer of satisfaction knowing that I hadn't been that far off with my original suspicions.

"Yes. He waited a while before quietly opening his door. He went down the stairs to the basement where there was a delivery entrance used for moving things in and out of the building. That's how he got out without anyone seeing him leave."

"All that effort to kill an innocent man.," I said softly. "And that's what they had planned for me too, wasn't it?"

"I'm afraid so." Andy said. "We know now that Helen saw you as a threat to her plan. She had Fred try to scare you off with the car and when that didn't work, she had him make the threatening call. When you showed up at the library, she realized you weren't going to stop your questioning, so she decided to lure you up to her apartment where Fred would be waiting with the bat."

"But if you didn't know any of that before last night, why were you trying to reach me?"

"We were concerned for your safety. And, knowing your persistent interfere...uh, sorry, interest in Helen, we wanted to make sure you remained safe and stayed away from her until we sorted this out."

"Andy and Brian originally were on their way just to question her," Milt chimed in. "But when they arrived and Helen opened the door, she denied that you were there while I kept insisting you had to be there. After that, well, everything just escalated rapidly."

"I'm surprised that she let you in."

"I'm sure she didn't want to, but at some point she had no choice," Andy said. "Your husband had already been knocking at her door for a minute or two before we arrived. When we got there we told her we'd break the door down and it would be worse for her if she didn't cooperate. She finally opened the door and was surprisingly calm at first. Then as we bombarded her with questions as to where you were and what we believed she had done, she started yelling, kicking and screaming. She kept insisting that you weren't there and that we were trying to frame her."

"Would you have left?" I asked meekly, realizing how close I came to joining Sol in the hereafter.

"We didn't have a search warrant, so we wouldn't have been able to do too much more if she told us to leave. Fortunately your husband saw your earring on the floor. That gave us probable cause and the rest, as they say, is history."

I closed my eyes. This was all so unbelievable. If it wasn't for the pain still throbbing in my head, I would have been convinced that it really was a bad dream after all.

When I opened my eyes, Milt was looking at me with such concern that I forced a smile, reassuring him that I was all right.

"You're my hero," I said in a groggy voice. "See Milt, getting personally involved isn't so bad. If you hadn't done anything when Andy called, or if you had left it for the police, it wouldn't have turned out nearly as well."

"Good try, Sadie, but nothing doing." Milt was about to launch into another tirade about my persistent interfering when I held up my hand. "I'm only kidding," I said as I felt my eyes struggling to give in to sleep. "I know now how stupid it was for me to have walked right into her trap."

"Actually Mrs. Maven," Brian interrupted. "You helped us a lot with this case."

I heard their voices from far away. "All I ever wanted to do was help my neighbors," I whispered in a feeble attempt to respond.

"Well, be that as it may," Andy added before he and his partner started to walked out. "We thank you for your help. In spite of everything I said to you over the last few days, you did good. Real good. In fact," he winked at Milt, "maybe you should consider becoming a private investigator for the department."

Oy! I thought as I finally drifted off. Private investigator for the department? Permanent involvement! They had to be kidding. After all, that would be just positively insane!

EPILOGUE

Two weeks later, Morris Rubenstein sent around a notice calling for a tenant meeting for Wednesday evening. Milt and I went together. Mrs. Pinsky was already there.

In fact, while I had been busy getting my head and body healed, my friend Mrs. Pinsky had been busy preparing daily meals for Mr. Rubenstein.

At first she'd stop by with a little casserole, a pot of chicken soup or some of her famous strudel. Then Mr. Rubenstein began stopping by her apartment, presumably to return the dishes. That gradually led to him staying for dinner. They'd watch television, play a little cards and eventually she started taking short walks with him every now and then.

Mrs. Pinsky and Mr. Rubenstein became quite an item. They were often the topic of discussion among various tenants in the building. They were also quite cute together and even Milt admitted I was right about their budding romance.

At the meeting that evening, Mr. Rubenstein announced to the tenants that upon Sol's untimely death, the ownership of the apartment went to him. This elicited a great deal of surprise and questions. He raised his hand to quiet the large group assembled in the lobby.

"This is my home," Mr. Rubenstein was saying, warming to his speech. "I wouldn't want to move, so why should you be forced to? Therefore, this is what I've decided to do."

I could tell he was enjoying himself. For a man of few words he had certainly came out of his self-imposed exile with panache.

"My sister's son, Leonard Freidken, will come out from California next month to take over the running of this apartment building. I'll be the owner in name only. I'm too old to run anything anyway. Nothing will change. If you have rent control, it stays the way it was and if you don't, we won't raise your rent."

A big cry went up from the tenants, a jubilant cry this time. Then applause erupted as the tenants moved forward to personally shake his hand and praise him for his thoughtfulness and good will.

As for Helen Brunner and Fred Porter, they went away for a long time. John moved to Tennessee to be with his family and the Dudley brothers remained gainfully employed in Utah. Their comment, overheard by one of the tenants, had nothing to do with the murder. The opportunity for full time employment had been so tempting they had decided to leave without giving notice to their current employers, hence the reference to getting into trouble when that was discovered.

With all the loose ends neatly tied up and my health and well being back on solid ground, I was, once again, a happy person.

"This was a far cry from that first tenant meeting," I told Milt as we returned to our apartment.

"I'll say." He took my hand and squeezed. "I hope it stays that way, too."

And it did. It was actually as close to a happy ending as you could get.

As for me, well, I put all this P.I. stuff away, at least for a while. But truth be told, looking back at it all now, I have to admit that being right there in the middle of a police investigation was particularly interesting and an absolutely, positively incredible adventure!

Made in the USA
San Bernardino, CA
31 August 2014